Fragments of the Mirror

A Heart Warming Series of Short Stories

Michael Wallace

Ring the bells that still can ring

Forget your perfect offering

There's a crack in everything

That's how the light gets in

Leonard Cohen

"The truth was a mirror in the hands of God. It fell, and broke into pieces. Everybody took a piece of it, and they looked at it and thought they had the truth."

Rumi

Fragments of the Mirror

Copyright © 2015 Michael Wallace

All Rights Reserved

Published by Ladder to the Moon Publications.
ISBN: 978-0-9756994-8-5
Mailing: PO Box 1355 Kingscliff, NSW 2487
WEB: www.laddertothemoon.com.au

INDEX

Fragments of the Mirror

Author Intro:

There is a Hindi story of how the God, Rama, carried a large mirror, but it fell from his hands and shattered into a million pieces. Each piece was a Soul, and it's journey was to become complete once more, part of the whole from whence it came.

These small tales represent a journey towards wholeness. I see each story that comes off the typewriter as a small piece of this greater mirror, one that, hopefully, reflects something of the divine back to you. I gather the broken bits of each fractured soul I write about, and in telling their story I trust you will be able to put them back together.

This compilation comes from a time in my youth, a time when I had absolutely no idea about anything. I had nothing of value to offer anyone, no money in the bank, no assets other than my curiosity, no job to speak of, and not much future it seemed. And, though I did not fully realise it at the time, my health was in a very bad way. I was looking at death every day in the mirror.

To give a little background: At age 17 I had walked into a Townsville Hospital (Queensland, Australia) with a temperature over 106 F. I only managed to get there because I was feeling better that day. The doctor there declared, "You can't be walking, let alone be alive!"

I had contracted a disease, the first version of the SARS virus, as we know it today. (Hong Kong Flu) Most teenagers who got this died in their sleep. I had the good sense to realise I needed to sleep sitting up, and this is apparently what saved me.

Surviving the virus was one thing, but the aftermath was unexpected and difficult. At age 17, I could run 10 miles in under 50 minutes. I had a 44" chest with 22" upper legs. Yet 3 years on, by age 20, I had shrunk to a mere slip of a soul who weighed just over 7 stone, and who could easily fitted into girls 24" jeans. If I ate anything, I threw up acid.

This went on for years, and I found it easier to just not eat. I should have been dead, really, but writing these stories kept me alive. I wrote every evening after getting home from work. I wrote a story a night, and though many of them were rubbish, as you would expect, it gave me a reason to be alive. Many years on, I was going through an old box that had been stored at my sisters warehouse, and these tales you now hold were discovered. I had forgotten I had written most of them.

So, these selected vignettes mostly come from this period. What you have here represent a coin toss of the better stories from my past. All of this came out a deep desire, a compulsion, an urgent need to write. I may well have been dead come the next morning, and I wanted to leave something that would tell the world I had been here, something that said I had some value. These stories are largely biographical, either from first hand experience, or from first hand accounts. Even the analogies, such as the "Dented Bucket", are based on people I have met. They are all coloured to suit the gist of the tale, yes, but essentially all are true. Even, or perhaps most especially, the fairy tales. They are true to their essence, which is far more important than being factually correct.

Purely through happenstance, the first part of this book focuses on issues of death and dying, the middle rests on people who are in between choices, and the last part follows on with what comes of the choices we make, and where they lead us. For me, this was a serendipity of sorts.

Regardless of the quality, or otherwise, the act of writing is what gave breath and life to me. It was not just my reason to survive; it gave me a warmth that made surviving worthwhile. It gave an inconsequential person with a nothing job some purpose worth living for.

But please, don't look through these tales and see the cadaverous 7 and a 1/4 stone twenty-two year old typing away on his ancient 1904 Remington. For myself, it wasn't like that at all. In the mirror, on the rare occasion I noticed myself there, I looked perfectly fine. To my eyes I was possibly a little too fat. And if you could have seen inside me, at that time, you would have seen I was HUGE. I was large with the weight of my stories. My heart glowed with every bend and twist in a tale, and it was the joy of writing that set it free.

A simple understanding drove all of this: *All people want is a good story.* We all have enough seriousness and suffering and silent vicissitude. Newspapers crowd our heads with what's wrong; TV fills us with lack of consequence; yet a good book, a good story, lights up the imagination. And when lit with a true flame, our imagination becomes a personal magic carpet ride, one that takes us out of the rut of the day to day, away from the millwheels of circumstance, and gives us a journey to somewhere interesting.

The truth is that these stories took me away from my pain. And I can say with certainty that they worked for me, because I am still here. So, I trust there will be a tale or two in this collection that you like. Ideally you will find a story in these pages that may mean something more to you than the letters and words that went into making them. Enjoy!

M. Wallace Jan 2015

SPENCER

Who can speak of what happens within the sacred bonds of the family? Well, when it came to the Eriksson's, everyone in Spencer, it seemed.

People said that the source of the concern was the family itself, yet reality begs me to say that the beginning of this drama was really one Mrs Emily Houve, a Dutch immigrant of some 50 years standing in the town. She was neighbour to the Eriksson's and a tremendous reservoir of information about all things Spencer. In other words, she was the town gossip. Naturally, she was interested in everyone's business but her own, yet the Eriksson's formed the highest agenda on her list. No greater enthusiasm, mixed with venom, could be found in her voice than when she spoke about her unfortunate neighbours.

Specifically, her enthusiasm for Irma Eriksson and the sheer, unadulterated venom for her miserable son, René.

"Yes" Emily spoke into the telephone as if it were an old, dear friend. "It's Six O'clock and he's off. Poor Irma, that ungrateful wretch is leaving her all night on her own, again. And after all she does for him. I know I should turn a blind eye, but how can I? You can hear her protesting her treatment sometimes, but I swear I have seen him drug her with some sort of witch potion that puts her to sleep. Why? Just so he can go out. But does she even complain to me? No, the woman is a saint. What a curse that lay-a-bout useless child has been for her."

The silhouette of Mrs Emily Houve stood against the dull lamp in her lounge. Outside, the soft glow of the summer, and the fading evening light showed the lazy son walk out to the pier where his boat would be fired up.

The voice on the other end sympathised, as it had done for many, many years (even though the sympathy had long departed). Even if you don't want to hear what is being said, you say little. Spencer is a small town, set on the

---

Hawkesbury River in Australia, and you had to make sure you kept your friends close because if you didn't, come tomorrow they wouldn't be talking to you, they would be talking about you.

A boat fires up, Emily flinches. She can't see it, but she knows. Rene' is off to town again. And slowly the engine fades from the night air.

Such a quiet, invisible village was Spencer. Weekends brought a modicum of life to the place, enough to stir the dust, as people would say. Being just two hours from Sydney meant that motor cycles, out for the bends and turns of the old highway, would rally around the local pub on the weekend. Sunday's and casual tourists would fill in the other empty spaces on the river as people rolled out their picnics. But the weekdays were as silent as a funeral parlour. You saw little but the passage of passing gossip. Now, in these twilight hours, that particular form of traffic moved to the telephone lines.

It is true that Emily Houve had been a nurse, and that she had dedicated her life to helping others. It is also true that she felt it was her personal and well-deserved right to discuss matters of relevance with other local people of importance regarding the general well-being of the town. René Eriksson was clearly a case that threatened the moral integrity of the place, thus the well-being of Spencer was at stake. This is why he had become her main focus.

True, also, that René was the only man in town to remain unmarried, and be under the age of 50. Sadly, it was also a fact that Petra Mantovski loved him in that desperately unrequited manner so suited to romance. Poor girl, over 40 now and still childless, probably still a virgin. (by Emily's estimation) Youth had faded like sheets too long in the sun. Her crispness had gone, yet Petra's strange enthusiasm for the boy down the street remained unabated. And why? He had taken the silly girl to her coming-out ball, what, a quarter a century ago now? Stupid girl. She had idolized him ever since, despite his obvious indifference.

How time passes in Spencer. 50 years since Holland, it could have been yesterday. Was it really 25 years since Petra's first embrace or that nasty child Rene'? It seemed like moments ago! 24 years since the death of John Eriksson, and the start of the suffering for poor, dear Irma. And 23 years since the start of the shiftless existence of that nere-do-well son. Imagine, all that time and money wasted on University? A fully accredited lawyer for God's sake, and he had not done one moment of work in his whole life.

Yes, he helped the locals with legal things, but he was too weak to go to court for them and always referred people to some fellow in Gosford. Spineless, Emily judged him in her simple way.

That's what got her the most, the cowardice. It was bad enough that he sat in his mother's house his whole life, or at least since he returned from Law School, but he didn't even have the gumption to open an office in town. He did nothing useful with his life, that's what infuriated Mrs Houve the most.

She had told her husband often enough that he should go over and straighten the boy out. It may have been worth something back then, just after the father had died. It may have been the tonic the boy needed, but Piers was a weak-kneed jellyfish himself and refused to even try to help poor Irma. "Not my problem" he would say as he munched toast in the morning. Then he would pick up his paper, saying "Not yours, either". She hated him for that, bless his soul. But he was dead now, and it WAS her problem.

Piers had never sat in the Café each week and heard the sorrow and suffering the woman went through. Week after week of cleaning, cooking, washing, even mowing the lawn. All for the no-good lay-a-bout, but she never once complained. He would not even take her shopping, and she was in no fit condition to travel to the main town all on her own, fragile as she was. Always she had to order what she wanted and pay to have it delivered. Miserable useless child.

Irma was a saint, so humble, always saying how she was simply happy to serve the good Lord in any way he chose. "Maybe he will find a good wife?" she would say. One who would willing take that that burden on? No girl but simple ignorant Petra is that stupid, Emily thought to herself.

René Eriksson never even went to church. He never went to a town social, never mingled, never sat down the bar with the men. He was a loner. Every night without fail he would take his boat down the river, no doubt to fall into some lover's arms or the embrace of some drug party, or to cultivate some secret crop. Each morning he was apparently back home, yet Emily never once heard him return despite the fact she was always up at dawn. He would sleep all day, and go out again to his friends that night. René was a puzzle. 46 years he had lived in Spencer and no-one knew anything about him. What was the secret?

"The Secret" had fuelled Emily's curiosity for years now, and had become a part of her character. It was when she had organised to hire a detective to follow René and see what he was up to (She was sure he must be dealing drugs) that her husband finally put his foot down. "Spending good money chasing other people's business, woman? I'll have you on the street before you go wasting my hard earned cash on this rubbish."

He even went and spoke to René to make sure! How completely embarrassing. Piers had become so intent on the matter of stopping her that it had become a condition of his will. That stupid, ignorant man, bless his soul. He put the property and finance into a family trust that gave her a regular and comfortable income for life, on the single condition that she left the Eriksson's business completely alone. Lord forgive her for the thought, but why did Piers want to punish her from the grave?

Of course, it was René who helped Piers draw up the clauses. That was just another reason to hate him. But, Piers (dear, foolish man) had been gone 5 years now. It was a serviceable enough time to start enquiring into how she might end this silly will business he dreamt up, and get her hands on the money.

But not just for herself? Poor Irma was also trapped in a strange will. She had asked about the money, but Irma, the saint, had no idea and did not care. Her wretched son looked after the details. Why, he may even one day kill her for the house if Emily could not act to save her.

After much tracking down Emily, uncovered a fellow called Peter Davies. He was a dark horse, someone outside the normal coral of lawyers, and just what she needed. What was more he gave his first advice free. Well, the price was right. He was also a solicitor of the shady variety, with many inclement clients. Exactly what she needed. It was just that he only worked evenings, which beyond being strange meant a ferry and a coach and a very late night of it. She booked the appointment regardless.

By report, the man also helped the homeless and the street children, so he lived the hours they did. A very noble Soul, thought Emily, and so convenient because he also took Legal Aid. A bit of a pain to go see, however. Even so, her conversation with the receptionist confirmed that the first interview was free. So there would be no records, no charge, and free advice. So she could find out where she stood, at last. This would hardly go against the terms of the will, would it?

Such a happy coincidence that her local bowls team would be over in Gosford that week for a State round and had offered her a bed at their hotel if she were too tired for the travel back. So with everything organised she had confirmed the appointment with the fellow's secretary. She had her papers in order, along with her husband's will, so finally she could find out if it was all properly legal. How could it be legal to stop a friend helping out another friend? With that sorted, then she could get the fellow to help out her long suffering neighbour.

Soon. Soon enough.

CONVERSATIONS:

Conversation has been going on ever since man first learned to speak. Conversation is the reason we learned to speak, and conversation of itself still impels us, drives us, draws us to society. Our conversations are what govern us.

No doubt such deep thoughts were far away from Emily and Heidi as they sat in Café Brussels the next day. Their mutual distaste for all things Slavic had stopped that day, for poor Petra Mantovski appeared to have had been forced to move to Gosford. Can you imagine? All her life in Spencer, and now she must live in the city because her local government position had been shut down.

She had been the teacher in the local school for so many years, but the children had all grown old, and the school was to be closed. So that was it for Petra.

"Bureaucracy is an evil thing." Heidi said as they sat drinking tea, hands resting on the faded laminate top table. The tin legs of the chair against the linoleum gave a dull, wax killing tone. Their pavlova was jabbed and tortured by the fork, as the women muttered against the cold indifference shown their village. A closing school meant a dying town. "Evil" said Emily. "It's another step towards the dark."

Café Brussels was the centre of their collective universe. Though both were European by birth, the women had never been to Belgium and had no concept at all of small intimate coffee houses. The women rarely left Spencer, and only then for visits to hospital and the like. As a result of a natural osmosis, they had precious little of German or Dutch left in them now. Like iron filings too long on the magnet their imagination now bent around all things Spencer. The dichotomy of a cafe' named after ancient Europe clashing with 1960's Australian Kitsch never even touched them

"Governments" snorted Emily, "After they get your vote, they don't care. It all figures and statistics, and we don't count for much in their books. Poor

Petra, suffering a lifetime of waiting for that useless René, and now tossed like a rag on the heap."

Heidi, of course, agreed. "You know, she's so brave. Just yesterday she said to me," the two women leaned forward conspiratorially "She said that she would be GLAD to leave Spencer and live in Gosford"

"She was always the brave one, always putting on the bright face so we don't feel bad." spoke Emily. "She was like that even as a child, she was. Always brave. This town was so much the better for her talent and hard work. Why she even taught my niece how to play piano, did you realise that?"

Of course, Heidi knew that, but she uttered a murmur of agreement to be sure. "Wonderful, talented soul." She said. Then, after a moment, she added "You know, we really should do something as a going away for the girl. Perhaps we could contact some of her old students, and have a get together?"

"It's a lovely, kind thought, Heidi my dear, but you KNOW what the problem will be." The sense of water dousing hot coals permeated Emily's voice. "It's not just finding the people, getting them back here, and organising it all. It's not just the selfish new generation who may not even care that their old teacher has been thrown on the waste basket of life, and who may not even bother turning up. It's the food to cook, the music to play, the venue to sort out, and the lack of time. The girl is leaving in just over two weeks, after all."

"Well, maybe we could have a small get together with the locals. A dinner to just say goodbye and thanks. A simple affair." Heidi compromised. "What do you think?"

"An excellent notion dearest Heidi. I am sure everyone will be delighted. But there is an obvious concern!" The manner and tone used meant only one thing: Him!

"Look, he's away every evening partying it up. We can just have the meal after 7pm. That way we spare poor Petra having to see how much time she has wasted here, waiting on him." Heidi's German obviousness showing through in all its practicality!

"Of course Heidi dear. How stupid of me not to think about this. Shall we make a date at the village hall for a fortnight's time, then?"

"Leave it to me, Emily. I will make sure everyone knows, except René, of course. But should we invite Irma? You know how devoted she is to her son, for reasons I can't explain, but maybe she would be hurt if she knew we excluded him?"

Emily was pained to think that she could not invite her old friend, but Heidi was correct. And after all, no one ever saw Irma out after dark. As soon as her son left, everything got locked up tight. Irma had hardly left the house since her husband passed away, God rest his soul, and apart from trips to the Dentist or Doctor her only other stopping point was this café. "You are quite right Heidi dear. Please mention to people that Irma is not to be told. Everyone will understand, considering how poor Petra has suffered from that wretched René."

All the way back home Emily thought about how badly the curse of the Eriksson's had affected so many people. It disturbed the calm of village life. "It's a damn cancer" she spat out, angry, frustrated. And what do you do with Cancer? You cut it out and free yourself from this poison. But how?

One thing was absolutely certain, as long as René got a free ride on his mother's tailcoat, he was never going to leave town.

CONVERSATIONS: Part Two

"I don't know why you put up with him Irma. Toss him out, get rid of him. You would be so much better off on your own."

"My darling Emily" chortled Irma at the notion, "I do love you, but I love my son as well. Really, it doesn't matter any more. I have become used to it. All children use their parents, and I know you can't understand not having had any yourself, but that's just how it is."

"Irma" Emily retorted, "Having children or not has nothing to do with it. He uses you, he's a parasite. I live in anguish every day knowing how you suffer, ever since ... " Emily was going to mention John's name, but she had long ago learned how unwise this was. Just the mention of his name, even so many years after, sent Irma off into a wild uncontrolled emotional fit. She would cry "Why Why Why" at the mere mention of her departed husband. Emily bit her lip…

"Ever since René started going out each night to that place down the river, Irma dear," Emily half lied. It was true, though. René had started going there immediately after the father had died.

"It's not what you were going to say, was it?" Irma asked accusingly.

"Yes, yes" Emily rallied. "It's just that I don't even like to mention your Son's name, it upsets me so."

"Oh, I see. Well I can understand that. Certain things upset me emotionally as well, my dear. We must all try our best to keep in charge of these little upsets, mustn't we?"

She's so strong, thought Emily. Even though she knows what I was going to say, she is keeping herself calm. The woman is a SAINT. "You are absolutely correct my dear," Emily replied with a hint of the stoic. "Still there are some things in life that we should not have to bear!"

"Oh Emily, Emily!" Irma moved to comfort her old friend. "It's not so bad, really it's not. You get used to things, you really do. But you are right, some things should NOT be born, but once they are my dear, once they are, that's it. It can't be changed. Life is what it is. Our lives are not the easiest, but compared to children starving in Africa I couldn't in front of the Good Lord dare to complain about MY lot, could I?"

"Certainly, it can be hard, but just as much as God made rocks for us to sit on, other hard and uncertain fates serve his purpose as well. I will not argue with God's will, and neither should you." Irma spoke with finality.

Emily felt chastised, yet even as she felt the truth of what her friend said it made her feel even greater anger. How could such an understanding saint like this have to suffer the continuing torment of a wastrel like her son? But Irma was right. God's will is his own. However a few queries to this lawyer could not be seen as an intrusion into God's plan. Indeed, perhaps it WAS God's way of doing things?

The simple note written with a trim, gold letterhead confirmed the appointment. It had only just come in the morning post, but she dare not show it to Irma. This Peter Davies fellow had been so gracious and gentle that she was surprised. He wrote in perfect longhand, not typed, and addressed her directly as "My Dearest Mrs Houve". What a nice boy. She felt certain he was the key to unlocking this horrid puzzle they had all gotten locked into.

It is quite possible that by this time next week René would have to be answering some awkward questions, such as: How was the will of his father being disposed of? Where was he spending the money? Emily was certain a good solicitor would ferret the rat out of its nest. She had already forgotten the real reason was to sort out her OWN issue with her husbands will.

More and more Emily realised that the son was most likely abusing any benefit left his mother by the father. This was the real reason he hung on. He wants to bleed her dry, she thought, just like a vampire. "No better than a vampire" she muttered to no-one as she made her way home.

Then it struck her! He was out all night, stayed home through the days, lived off others! Yes, he was a vampire alright, of the worst sort. She just needed the right bit of legal hickory wood to put an end to this evil, for everyone's sake.

A LEGAL MATTER:

The week had passed quickly. Plans for Petra's farewell proceeded along quite smoothly. Of course, everyone felt wrong about having to leave poor Irma out of things, yet it would go so hard on her if she found out.

Emily had gone with the bowls team to town, as she felt too anxious to travel on her own at night, and after all, it would be nice to spend a day shopping. Yet it did not start well. Heidi was completely off her game. The team had lost badly and was out of the competition before lunch. This was not the cause of the dark mood, but mostly the result of one. All knew why Emily was there, and what she was risking if she was found out. For herself, she had deep doubts arising. Was she doing the right thing?

Year after year her husband had told her to mind her own business in regard the Erikssons. Piers was no fool, but he could not nor would not understand her view on this matter. For him it was simple and uncomplicated: Their side of the fence is their business, and don't interfere with the neighbours.

When she complained that he did not understand, he simply said that he had no right to understand what a neighbour does, or how they live. All that counted was whether the garbage was put out, that the fences were kept in good order, and that peace existed. "Go sticking your nose into another families business, wife, and it'll get snipped. Families that hate each other, they're everywhere. But point it out to them and they'll hate you, and moreover blame you for their problems. Trust me woman, I am right on this one. Stay well out of it."

His voice had haunted her all day, had haunted her ever since she made the appointment, but it was just questions she was asking. Questions were not going to ruin anyone's life. All she wanted was for a good, quiet lawyer to ask probate to check out that all was in order, and if it was, well that would be that. If it wasn't? Well, this was also well and good. At least it would be known. She had a Christian duty and a Christian obligation, and after all, there was no charge. It was a legal aid matter.

She had paid her dues to society, and certainly poor old Irma had, so it was fair that society pay a little to help poor Irma. It was a small favour returned. Poor Irma. Poor Petra. Nothing was their fault, yet both were long suffering, Yet neither of them had ever complained, even for a moment. She had a Christian duty to protect the rights of the innocents, a Christian and moral duty.

Heidi was better when they got back to the hotel room that afternoon. Even so, she didn't feel much like eating, and neither did Emily, so after a cup of tea the excuse was made of a little business to attend to, and the two parted company: Heidi to read a book, and Emily to discover one of those odd, little twists of fate.

The afternoon dragged by in shopping malls. Fabrics were looked at, silverware inspected, and more cups of tea were had until, finally, the evening began to fall and exhausted from the long day, Emily finally called over a taxi to take her to the appointment.

The building was very plain, and not in a good area of town. Emily rushed from the cab, pressed the buzzer and anxiously moved through the door when the slight "click" told her it had been unlocked.

A receptionist took her personal details, and asked a little of why she had come. "I would prefer to discuss this with the lawyer, if you don't mind." she snapped, somewhat indignant that this slip of a girl could be so rude. The receptionist quietly explained that in this practice things worked a little differently from most.

She spoke of how they deal with a good many very unpleasant cases, things that were from the lowest end of society, and that there were a lot of people to see. Details NOW saved the solicitor a lot of time. Very few cases went to court here, and most problems were solved by communication, and trust was the key in communication. "You have to trust us, Mrs Houve. Peter (the Lawyer) does a lot of negotiating with Police, organising compromises that keep people out of jail and instead doing some sort of service to society. We have a lot of domestic violence cases, Ma'am and we need to know what we are looking at."

"That may well be so, young lady, but I am here on a simple matter of probate."

"I am sorry," the girl apologised. "We tend to only get the cases other lawyers don't want, you know, the really messy ones. Are you sure this is the right practice for you?"

"Young lady, the man is a solicitor, is he not?"

"Of course, but …"

"No buts. I have come quite some distance to see this fellow and that is what I am going to do. You may tell him I simply wish him to make discreet enquiries about whether a probate matter is in order."

"Certainly Madam. You are the recipient, or is it the question of a relative here?"

"Neither my dear. I am simply making an enquiry on behalf of my friend."

"Hmmm…" The young lady was very efficient and did not like wasting time. "Are you aware Madam that only family members or recipients of a will have a right to bring a will into question?"

"Young woman!" Emily almost shrieked. ""You get in there and tell that young whatever-he-is fellow to get out here and see me! I do NOT need advice from a secretary."

The door to the inner office clicked open, another automatic lock, and from the darkened room inside a voice called out. "Send her in, Louise. I will speak to her."

Emily stared smugly at the girl as she stalked past. Fully in charge of herself now she walked into a darkened room, and immediately felt for the light switch. "I can't see" she said as she flicked it on. "You don't have to worry young man, I am not one of your criminal types. There's no need to hide from … RENÉ!" she shrieked.

THE TRUTH SHALL SET YOU FREE

Her knees fell from under her as the blood rushed from her now stark white face. Louise ran in, and with René they lifted her to the sofa, and put a pillow under her neck. Louise got some cold water and tried to revive the incoherently mumbling old woman.

It took some time for Emily to gather her wits. As she sat there in the foyer she was constantly amazed by the never ending stream of the most unsavoury and desperate characters you could hope to meet, or rather, avoid. She had refused the suggestion of an ambulance, but was too shocked to say much else. Finally as one fellow went into the dark room, she managed to ask, "Why is the room so dark?"

Louise looked up. René had briefly explained that this woman had been his neighbour in Spencer for all his life, and that no one in the town had any idea he worked here. It was a shock, and he asked her to take care of the dear old soul. "The room is kept dark for a number of reasons. Firstly because a number of our clients don't like to be seen as they discuss personal issues. People feel more private in the dark, and tend to be more open. It means we get to the point more quickly.

"Secondly Peter, or René as you know him, deals with the lowest types. Some are psychotic, which is why no other lawyer will touch them, and while he truly wants people to get a fair deal, he simply does not want them to be able to recognise him in the street should something go wrong.

"That's why he uses the pseudonym." Louise concluded.

"The what?" Emily asked.

"The false name, Mrs Houve."

"Oh" she replied automatically. It was all so very confusing. None of it made any sense at all. "Why doesn't he mow his lawn then?" She asked. Why she asked this odd question, even Emily herself didn't know, I suspect. Her mind had gone entirely blank but for this one, odd curiosity that presented itself through her shock.

Louise was a trained nurse, and understood well the effects of trauma. René had spoken to her extensively of his personal situation, and Louise was possibly the only one who had a full understanding of the details. "There is a lot you don't understand about René and his family, Mrs Houve."

"I have been their neighbour for 50 years!" she snapped back.

"Of course," Louise softened. "The reason René does not mow his lawn is because his mother insists she needs useful things to do around the house.

"You see, she has a very curious form of dementia that does not allow her to do anything in a confined space, but she can garden and mow happily. Do you know why she always gets her groceries home delivered?"

"Yes." Emily faltered, not really understanding what she was saying.

"Well, Mrs Eriksson can't shop either. It's a confined space. The condition is rare, because she can sit in a room happily, but she cannot clean, cook or DO anything without severe heart palpitations. Yes, she can go out, and order a cup of tea, but otherwise there is precious little else she can do, but she can work in the garden. So sad, isn't it? Her husband, may he rest in peace, apparently hoped the birth of René would snap her out of it but it just didn't work and she could not even look after him."

"The birth of René ?" Emily trailed off.

"Yes, well I guess you moved in just after the death of the second boy. Rene' was the only one of three to survive."

"I ... I didn't know she had other children?"

"Well, of course Irma would never mention it. She has this other phobia where the mention of anything close to her that has passed on sends her into deep shock."

"Yes... That's right... Irma... Yes she does that." Emily realised this was true, entirely correct... but it didn't fit with anything else.

"Well, apparently the doctor, you know Dr Phillips, the one who visits every other week?"

Emily nods vacantly. "Yes the doctor, such a nice man" He never did explain why he did so many house calls, come to think of it. He was another Spencer mystery.

"Well, he apparently said that the cause of the paranoia and dysfunction was linked to the death of the first two children. Cot death, you know. Very sad. It affected Mrs Eriksson to the degree that she could no longer do even the most basic tasks when indoors. Apparently all she can do inside the house is watch TV and eat prepared meals. She can't even make herself a cup of tea. It's just so difficult for everyone."

"TV? Yes, that's what she does." Yes, thought Emily, TV Soap Operas were her favourite. Irma knew all the characters.

René has often told me how you have been such a great friend to her over the years. He greatly appreciates the fact that you would meet with her so often at the Café. It allowed him to get things done around the house."

"Around the house?" queried Emily, weakly.

"Oh yes," Louise continued. "His mother would not allow anyone to do anything when her favourite shows were on. It would send her into a fit. The doctor wanted her put into a home but René would have nothing of it. He knew she could easily die with one of her fits, and an institution with its sense of isolation would certainly trigger them. Just the passing thought of another child dying could cause severe reactions. He knew she had to see him every day.

"Of course, it was not so bad when his father was still alive. His presence had a great calming effect on Irma, and she was quite happy to wait at home while he went out to work. René still had to do the housework, for the most part, but things were not so bad.

"Then, when John died, Irma fell completely to pieces. René could not practice law conventionally, so he started this after hours practice. This allowed him to sleep through the days when Irma watched TV, and he always gave her a pill to make sure she would be asleep before he left. It gave Irma the confidence that someone was always around.

"Instead of institutionalisation, René and the doctor opted for control with drugs. A sedative each night and they found some sort of enzyme for daytime that balanced out the emotions. It made her light-headed and prone to fantasies, but the wild rages where she would break everything in the house stopped. So she was permitted to stay at home, because she was no longer a risk to others or herself.

"Poor woman, but honestly, I feel sorrier for René. His whole life is governed by this one, mad woman. Still he manages to do an enormous amount of good regardless of the hurdles he confronts.

"At least he will inherit the house." Emily trailed off, so completely lost at this point that nothing made sense anymore.

"Inherit? Oh no, Mrs Houve. A certifiably insane person cannot inherit a property. The house was transferred into René's name at the death of the father, as the will said. Though for all the world, he's so rich he could live anywhere he wanted. But again, he can't move because his mother would not cope, and he didn't want to take her away from her friends, good friends like yourself."

The walls seemed to be closing in. Weird noise squealed in her left ear, as if something was trying to break into her mind. Her whole world picture was falling apart. René was a solicitor? René was rich? René looked after his mother? Nothing made any sense.

Something then snapped in Emily. Suddenly she saw the truth of it all. It all made sense now. The dark room, the night hours! What an evil trick they were playing on her! He wasn't a vampire, he was the Devil!

"You WITCH!" she screamed, leaping up and thumping the desk with a violence you could not imagine from a frail old lady. "Besmirching a good woman's name, a SAINT she is. The way you tricked me in here, lured me here! You, and your devil in there, will rot in hell. You will all burn at a fiery stake and I will laugh. Laugh. Liars and cheaters! Devils!"

She screamed as she fled the den of iniquity. Emily fled down the stairs, through the door, and out onto the street. The truck driver had no chance of stopping.

POST MORTEM:

The funeral was a simple affair. It was held the day before Petra was to leave Spencer, and we arrive to find her sitting to one side, talking quietly to René. His mother had completely lost her mind when she realised that her dear neighbour Emily was not there anymore. "Dead!" she screamed, all day, all night. For two days it continued, until at last she was able to go out to the café'.

Then the worst of all possible things happened, she overheard someone mentioning Petra's going away party and how people had to make sure no one told Irma. The violent fits returned. The death of Emily, the betrayal by the town, it was just too much for her fragile state. She would no longer watch TV but took to wandering out on the streets and accusing any people she saw of murdering dear Mrs Houvre.

Obviously she was picked up, and this time René had no say in the matter. Doctor Phillips assigned her to a dementia ward where, within days, she apparently forgot her son even existed. When he visited she had no idea who he was, though strangely she knew all the inmates, and called them by her favourite soap opera character names.

Petra expressed her sincere sympathy, but of course both of them were fully aware that the burden had finally been lifted. Inwardly she was happy he was set free from that old dragon.

"So, I am told that Piers had adapted his will before he passed on to ensure you got the entire estate when his wife passed on? Is that why Emily came to see you?"

"I have no idea, Petra. He long ago told me how fixated she had been over myself. And when I was arranging her care and the family trust business in his will, he wanted that strange clause about her enquiring over the Eriksson's put in. He said she would have spent all the money trying to prove I was imprisoning my mother, can you believe it? The poor deluded woman.

"But the money itself was of no interest. As if I need her money? Anyway it was a clear conflict of interest, so I have directed the funds towards research for my mother's condition. But, to yourself. I imagine you, too, are happy to finally be set free from Spencer?" he concluded.

"You and me both, yes indeed. (she sighed) This town has fallen into itself and there are too many memories here for me." said Petra.

"So, you are teaching in Gosford now, near my office of all places!" René noted wryly.

"Yes. It is odd how things can turn, isn't it? I am sorry to hear about your mother, but the loss of this old bag (indicating the coffin) can only improve the neighbourhood."

"Petra, let's not speak ill of the dead, yes?"

"Why not? She spent all her life speaking ill of others."

"Yeah, well. That's true. How have you been?"

"Fine, I guess."

"You know Petra, I don't know if you still prefer girls, but if you ever change your mind?"

"René, I told you 24 years ago, as much as I love you, I still prefer girls in my bed. Nothing personal, but if I change my mind, you'll be the first to know, OK?" They laughed.

The minister looked up, somewhat severely, then continued uttering some comforting words to friends and relatives. He spoke about the sadness of those who remain behind, and then came the inevitable drone about how from the dust, new seeds take root. The cycle of life, dust to dust, etc. etc.

The coffin of Emily Houvre went, with very few tears, into the ground.

Louise, the quiet receptionist who adored her employer, stood quietly off to one side, smiling with how everything had changed. Such an irony. The dead woman came to see a solicitor about sorting out her own and her neighbours. will, yet it was the cause of her own death, and the imprisonment of her friend.

A twist of fate? Or is it that fate just twists. Maybe now with his mother gone, maybe now Rene' will finally notice her.

As the last rites were spoken, the living were released from the dead.

The GREEN GLASSES - Part One

The very odd little man stood in the doorway of the shop where Albert had worked for years. Albert was oddly drawn to the fellow, and wanted to talk to him, but there were too many customers that day, and the day after, and even the day after that.

To his surprise, each day the strange man returned, and just stood there. But Albert was not paid to solicit business. If the man wanted something, he had to come and ask. The owner only paid him to stand behind the counter, not to prospect for business. Yet his curiosity was gaining ground over his natural sense of inbred employee carelessness.

On the forth day, finally the odd gnome-like creature solved the problem, and came forward to speak to him. Albert apologised for not being able to see him on earlier days, and asked what he might be wanting.

"Hmmmm? Me wanting, you think? I think not." The strange fellow said in a cryptic, heavily accented English.

"Oh dear" Albert said to himself, "Another salesman."

"I am not the owner of the shop. If you have anything you wish to sell you must come back and speak with him. Or I can give you his number, should you wish to call."

"Hmmm…" said the gnome in a curious ton. "No it is you I want to see. Or maybe I should say I want YOU to see? Do you think? I think you need these." His hand reached into a pocket of his tattered tweed coat and pulled out an old pair of spectacles. "Yes, I do think, I do think you want to try them on, yes?"

Albert was good at his job because he was quick to work out a new person. He always looked for little signs, or 'tells' as they are called. But this strange man was nothing like what he had ever seen. He was extremely short, maybe just 5 feet, and had this huge nose that bent and twisted in a way that was completely disproportional to the rest of his face. And the face! It had skin so dry it looked like old paper. The eyes though, dark and menacing, they stared right through you. Albert was completely naked before this man, and it embarrassed as much as it fascinated him. And yet there was something familiar about him. Something he already knew.

That was when he focused on what was in the fellow's hand. The odd, gnome-like thing was offering Albert a 1950's pair of Ray Bans, but emerald green in the lens and frame, rather than black. Albert's hand reflexed out. Who had told the man of his passion for collecting old sunglasses?

Then they were in his hand. Perhaps his desire for the new toy had tricked his mind, but Albert could swear the glasses put themselves in his hand. This could make him look too anxious, and drive the price up. "Really," Albert deferred, "I can't talk personal business while at work."

The gnome cut him off. "Try them on. They like you, I can tell. I am never wrong with these things, the glasses told me to come here, they want you to know them."

Well, the Ray Bans were in his hands already, so what harm could it do? Albert had always respected a good salesman, and this guy was the best. It no longer mattered that the price was going to be high, these were the rarest pair of Ray Bans he had ever seen. Absolutely unique and in pristine condition. So he put them on: And for the first time in his life, Albert saw everything.

EVERYTHING!

It was hard to describe it, but for the first time in his short existence. Albert deeply saw just everything. The sunshine outside was brilliant and sparkling. It came through the glasses with joy, freedom and such a love for life that he forgot entirely where he was.

The plants in the street outside seemed to effervesce, and birds that flew by were a stream of rainbows sparkling with delight. In his amazement, he saw the gnome moving out from the shop, only now it was no longer a short, ugly creature, but a lithe, athletic figure of sinew and power, who wore flowing, black robes.

Albert wanted to call out, but the rapture of these incredible glasses had him, and all he could do was watch the amazing parade of life move past. He was entirely and completely transfixed by the moment, and said nothing as the once-was-a-gnome man slipped past the shop window like a black fish moving out into a deep ocean. The world had shifted gear, and turned inside out.

Everything outside was brilliance and vigorous, yet when he brought his gaze back inside the shop, everything was grey, dull and banal. Uninspiring, empty, vacant, insipid and boring were the words to describe his workplace.

Empty? The shop was full of customers before he put on the glasses. Albert took them off, and there they were, several of them, looking at him with dull interest as they waited to be served. Albert glanced back out to where the gnome had gone, and he caught the last glimpse of what was clearly a short, ugly man again. And outside was just outside once more.

He put the glasses back on. Immediately the customers vanished, and the incredible world of delight opened up again, filling his heart with wonder. Hue, radiance and beauty dripped from every piece of life outside the store, while the shop itself remained lifeless.

Without comprehension, and in shock, Albert shook himself from this extraordinary event. He still had this job to do, so he took the glasses off and slipped them into his pocket. The customers looked at him oddly, but he went through the routine of service. Yet all the time he was not there, and could only imagine what it would be like getting outside during lunch hour and seeing these glasses do their magic without interruption. Then again, perhaps the magic would not last? Maybe he must rush out now and grasp the nettle! What to do?

The simple shop boy had little to lose. He put the glasses back onto his nose, and apologised to the customers (that he could no longer see) saying he would be back in a moment. He stepped outside the door, and was never to be seen in that shop ever again.

A NEW WORLD

It was truly a world reborn. Life sprouted from every pore of his existence as Albert realised for the first time since he had been a child just how wonderful life was. Everything was alive! Everything except the tired, worn-out shells of humanity that whispered along as ghosts on the streets of gaiety and sunshine.

Adults were like grey shadows, while the children were bright sparks of happiness. They seemed to recognise him, and invited him to laugh and play and sing. Soon he realised that everything close to nature sang with delight. The children glowed with rapture, and their little voices were a choral symphony to his ears. Flowers exuded a romance, and their fragrance coloured the space between the atoms with subtle shifts of indescribable beauty. The very air he breathed seemed alive and vibrant, ringing with bells. Yet when a vehicle came past, the grey energy it emitted dulled all around it, and painted that part of the world with a matt grey. But the breeze would pick it up and take it away as soon as the car passed by.

Albert went to the park, delighting in this incredible new vision, and wondering how long it might possibly last. He stopped every now and then to lift the glasses, and there it was, the world he knew. It had become incredibly ugly to him. Then a curious awareness arose, a paranoia crept in. And he began to ask himself the obvious: What was this for? Where had the gnome gone? Why had he simply given him these incredible glasses?

There was no answer, but the glasses HAD leapt into his hands. Maybe he just needed to accept it? Somehow, perhaps it was right for him to have this gift, but something else nagged at the back of his mind that it wasn't right.

Albert's attention fell increasingly towards the dull grey ghosts that, once the glasses were lifted, became people again. Children were exempt from the contempt of the glasses. The harsh critique of the spectacles was reserved for man-made things and adults, though as he put them on and took them off, it appeared that old people often seemed to be OK. Why?

He bought an apple from a street vendor, and went back to the park to sit and contemplate. He bit into the apple, and it was an apple, but as he slipped the glasses back on, a profusion of sense filled every corner of his being. It was not just an apple, but an incredible proof of life that coursed through his veins. Albert could see in minute details how the process worked. The apple was life, and from it, molecules of iridescent light sent a radiance through every cell that the atoms of the apple touched. It enlivened his whole being, while inside his mouth was alight with the fire of sweet truth.

But take them off, and there was nothing. It was just an apple once more. Put them back on and streams of energy pulsated through his heart, bursting like fireworks in his mind, while his tongue tingled like it was being stroked by the caress of a lover. Even the sumptuous clarity of the word "apple" rang true. He what it meant to be APPLE. There were no words to describe it, just the experience of being that said it all.

Even as he savoured the essence of this fruit, he studied it, became it, lived with its experience. He knew this apple, and like a window to a universe of eternity, he also knew all other apples that had ever been. What's more, he could feel how every apple knew he knew, and that somehow the apples both knew and appreciated that he understood their purpose and truth.

In the back of his mind, something was saying how, in any other circumstance, he would have considered himself entirely, completely mad. Yet this experience was absolutely real, as unfathomably true as it was impossible.

More real than anything he had ever known. More real than any drug he had ever taken. More powerful than any love he had ever known, this deep insightful knowingness was something unique and clear. It was totally foreign, and yet it was HIM. It was all HIM.

The exploration of the apple had led him deeper inside himself. There was no end, no beginning, all was NOW. All just is as it is, was as it was, will be as it will be. There was only the singular, even though he could see the many. The plurality of experience of being here and being now coalesced into a flow that took him inside every drop that had ever existed in a sea of freedom.

Why, then, were there these vacant shapes of grey people walking by? In some cases, the shadows themselves vanished, leaving only a dull scent that slowed the flow of life as it moved past. Sunlight filled the void, giving some substance to the ghosts, yet the children were immune. Why?

Slowly some reasoning to this experience took hold. It was more like an imaginative leap into something, but a something that created a reality to anything it touched. Perhaps this power the glasses held would reveal to him a message, something he could understand?

With the inner question the outer scene altered in imperceptible but certain ways. The grey shadows revealed themselves as doubts and fears and uncertainty. He heard whispers from the dark inside these people, he saw the lies that had been believed and which now ruled the mind of that person. He felt the anguish of loss, and the fear of gain. Anticipation in youth had now faded to disconsolate expectation of misery, oh the misery, and all were running in their own debt, their own doubt in their self-worth.

Albert could see variations of this in all these shadows. Yet oddly the whole of the misery and suffering they experienced was usually pinned on just two or three small details. These were the small, false beliefs, and an insidious guilt that perverted the core energy inside these souls, and twisted itself upon itself. He suddenly saw with brilliant clarity that these beings were Suns that had fallen into themselves and were now in the process of becoming black holes.

And just as surely he saw that if he reached out to remove the pegs that held the misery in place, the fire from that Sun would suddenly reveal itself, and burn him. Albert had no idea how he knew, but he trusted the truth of the vision and did nothing. It was all so clear now.

Children were rich in life, some old folk had gone past the fears, but the masses, who were convicted with the belief in their mortgage and relationships and sufferings, were trapped.

It was too much, and Albert lowered the glasses for a moment. Life resumed its former normality. A beautiful woman walked past, and a deep-seated ancient urge took up within him. He wanted to follow her, and there no impulse but to do so. He wanted her to try on these glasses, and then they would make wild passionate love in the park. His heart raced before his mind could stop him. He would know no bounds, fear no consequence, and nothing would prevent him from this incredible experience of total life!

Yet when he approached the girl, putting the glasses back on, she too became a ghost. A lost ship on an endless sea. A shell, a whisp, a nothing. All attraction left and revulsion took its place. He was amazed he could ever feel such desire one moment, and such disgust the next. It was confusion. Questions began to emerge. Was he going to see life this way forever? Would he ever meet someone who he could share these glasses with?

Could he trust anyone else with the glasses? Surely someone would steal them, but if he could meet the right one, how incredible would it be? Inside he made a wish, a pact, a dream, an intent: and even as he made this promise, he knew it would be fulfilled. What were these incredible glasses?

His whole body knew it. The glasses were drawing the one he must love towards him. He could feel the other coming closer. He tingled with expectation of what was to come, and knew with certainty that she would come. They would meet, he knew it. Just as certain as he knew the apple, he knew this. But when, and where?

Albert stopped once more' He took off the glasses and asked himself what the apple really tasted like. He bit it once more, and the normality of the experience took over. The brilliance flooded away from his nerves. Normality crept up once more, and it confused him.

Quickly he put them back on, and the Green Glasses experience came rushing forward immediately. Tantalising, rich, exhilarating and rewarding. With no further thought he made his way back to the park to soak up this incredible gift.

Hours passed. It must have been hours because night had fallen and a chill had crept into the air. To Albert the eventide appeared as a flaming sword of violet painting his body with messages of eternity, yet some part inside told him he needed clothes. That was when he looked at what he wore, and to his shock he realised he was living inside a grey, drab house. His dowdy clothes reeked of convention, compromise, and lack of self. He was truly astonished that he could have ever chosen such unimportant fabrics, crumpled, drab and reeking of fear. He stank of fear! He swam in it with clothes like this. He had to get rid them and went to take them off.

Something stopped him. Then the light of a store caught his eye, and in the window some beautiful silk outfits shone like a lighthouse. That was what he needed. He had little money on him, but this didn't matter. He had life in his veins and he needed those clothes. He could not even see the salesman in the fluorescent ugliness of the store interior, but he could see the clothes clearly. They sang out to him. He didn't even need to try them on, because he could trust his body to pick the right size.

He collected a shirt, a suit, shoes and socks, a tie, some accoutrements, a splash of cologne and then left without saying a word to anyone. There was no one there, after all, was there? He did not hear the shouting, nor even realise he had smashed the store owner against a wall. He was too happy with his new clothes to notice those petty creatures. The glasses gave him the grace and power to move through life like it was sand through his toes. He felt greatness flowing from within. He WAS greatness, a demi-God, if such could exist.

Breathing deeply of the night air he flowed more than walked back to the park, where he found the fountain. As he washed in the water and got dressed Albert was amazed that the thin light of a crescent moon could hold such a lucid clarity, one that allowed so many things to come into sharp focus. "This is as a cat sees!" he realised, and with this he sensed the feel of silk around his skin. It became as close and as personal as an animals coat.

The fabric sang where it touched his skin. "I belong to you" it sang "I am a part of you!" The colour radiated into him, bringing an ever more resonant pulse of blood through his mind. The scent of the expensive perfume spoke of distant horizons, waiting for him. "I have no limits!" Albert exclaimed, forgetting completely that only hours ago he was a mere clerk in a shop. "I am truly free!"

Up till that moment Albert had never known freedom, never tasted its intoxication. He came to understand that he had been born for this moment, and this moment was made for him. He had always instinctively known of its possibility, and now could see why he was so bored with his life. How long ago now? It seemed eternity since he met the gnome. Who was that gnome? What a unique being. But then, HE was unique. Yes, the one that is Albert IS unique! Albert is the most unique uniqueness that ever was.

Maybe he was the starting point? Maybe he had been selected for some obscure reason because he was the first seed to sprout? The gentle moisture of the night air filled his being. It was all so true, so real, that even when he took off the glasses the remarkable sense of perpetual being-ness remained longer. The dull, conventional world was a dream he had experienced, and only now was he beginning to wake up.

It had all come to this point, where Albert was the new cause, the new being, the new start to everything. He remembered his earlier wish for a perfect woman, the one who would resonate in harmony with his awareness. A woman he could enliven, enrich and enlighten. Yes, his body was saying this was what he needed, and his heart, and his mind. All of him came into accord with this single desire, and he knew it would be fulfilled.

Like the bloodhound on the scent, his instinct picked up the trail. It took him to a nightclub, a seedy run-down affair that looked shades of black through his glasses, but away to the right down a darkened alley a bright light caught his vision. A cadaver of drunks were playing around, laughing, joking and more to the point: They were visible! Clear, bright and present in the moonlight, they shone like bells.

Albert was struck by the word "serendipity". No fear contained him, the glasses did not lie. "Ho!" he called out to them. They looked up, saw the stranger, and suddenly it was as the light was switched off. All life left them and they became grey, motionless ghosts.

What was this? Albert was shocked. What had happened? Had the glasses lied? Were they false prophets? Then the thought came through, he was a stranger. The drunks had thrown off the shackles of society and were free. In their own worlds they were Gods, but the stranger called and pulled them from their freedom so that they fell back inside themselves. Their inner Sun was extinguished. They turned back into ghosts.

A police whistle screams, aching his ears. Some kids are being held and searched. As the authority goes about its business, Albert sees the colour fade from the children. They are learning to be adults. The police are not dull grey like the rest, they are solid black. Soaking up the resonance of fear their actions have created, they grow denser and firmer. Albert is watching from what seems a mile away. "POWER" a voice seems to deafen him with an intensity of stillness. Where did it come from?

The black started to fade, and it appeared that the boys had no drugs on them after all, and the police presence weakened, diminished and faded back to the collective dull grey. The effect spilled out to the energy of the trees, and all life seemed to go silent. The drunks stayed with their heads down, not making a sound. Each was shifting to its place within the mists of oblivion.

"Man is a tarnish on the face of the planet" thought Albert with what he once may have thought to be anger, but which was now just cold recognition. Man is a blot, a cancer, a disharmony, and an intrusion into the natural order. Only in nature does life flow easily and purely. But children were true and clear. Was this his mission? To bring the childlike energy back to the ghosts? Doubts began to assail him. Despite the clarity of the glasses, he asked what he could do. The world was large, he was small, all he had was a vision. Yet deep inside he knew he had to start, must decide, must find the woman, the Eve of his new world, his Eden.

He needed a bridge between the worlds of dreams and reality. He must have some certain point on which his life could revolve. Was this how Jesus had felt, he wondered? Did Jesus wake up like this one day, and did something like the Green Glasses happen to him? But how stupid, Albert then thought. He had no power to create miracles, or did he?

An old drunk lay in the gutter near where he walked. He could see the life force draining from him. The man was dying. "What if I imagine and place some of the incredible colour and joy I have been experiencing and place it all around him" Albert thought, "Maybe this would help?" So he allowed his thoughts to go to these places. He allowed the colours of life to flow through his heart, to come out from the park, and into the soul of the dying drunk.

Doorways opened, and he could look into the life of the dying man. He saw clearly the bitter setbacks that put him in the gutter, the failed marriage, the cruel backstabbing of his friends. Compassion welled up like a tide within, and washed over all. Everything of the man's life flowed past him, everything he had done and not done fanned out like a deck of cards.

The Green Glasses pulsed with power, and he saw the eyes of the man flicker. For a moment the drunk looked up. He said nothing, just stared, glancing everywhere and nowhere. And then it began. Albert could feel it, touch it, know it, sense it, savour it. Life came flowing in with waves of compassion. Slowly at first, but building larger and stronger. It was the heart beat of some distant universe he was feeling, and it grew moment by moment.

Vapour wrapped around him like mist, suffuse yet calm and beckoning. It crossed the space between himself and the drunk, and started to glow. "Is this love?" Albert asked himself. He knew it was, an essence so profound, so complete that there was nothing else but this moment that could contain it.

It was like the edge of a vast ocean. Step in and you would be gone forever. Albert knew he had to stand and allow it to come to him, flow through him, and go to the drunk. He was the reference point for Eternity, the chosen one and life had brought him to this place, this moment.

This amazing light reached out and flowed through the top of the man's head, down into his heart, out through his toes and fingers, then it simply broke through everything. Like a paper lantern being lit, the man took on a light of his own. He stood up, shining, brilliant and free, transparent to the divinity that flowed through him. He nodded severely towards Albert, and then the man transformed into a beam of sheer luminescence. This Soul was pulled up to the heavens, leaving only a phosphor trail behind.

Yet, Albert noted, the man had left his body behind. Dead.

For the first time since the gift of the glasses, Albert was scared. He was truly frightened, not by the power he had, but by what he might do with it. The glasses fell off into his waiting hands, and he sobbed with deep welts of pain echoing up from the confines of his heart.

He sobbed and sobbed, not knowing why. He knew nothing, he was worthless and everything he had ever known was gone. Anything he ever believed in was now ancient history, filed away in some forgotten chamber never to be seen again.

A MOMENT IN TIME

He sat there for who knows how long. The silk hung off him in the damn night air. The silent birds in the trees still breathed, but the strange and awesome fear of what he had been given had crashed through the prism of his reality, shattering it into razor edges of understanding.

He now knew his power was to liberate the fallen, but it was not what he had expected. Death was not supposed to come wearing silk robes, but black rags. Death was a skull, a threat, a fear, not a visitation of life.

Wasn't it?

Finally realising the horror of his situation, Albert went to throw the glasses away, but they did not leave his hand. He could not even say if he held them, or if they held onto him. They just stayed there, in his hand, waiting.

A hissing wail of sirens broke through his reverie. A driver careers out of control and sends the car into the river that runs beside the park. Without even thinking Albert's hand put the glasses on his nose, and a deep whir of energy took over. He was propelled by some force that flowed from his heart, and which brought him to the accident scene. There, once more, a man about to die.

Once more the deep compassion stirred up, and though Albert already knew the consequence, here was his true lover. Here was the Soul Mate he had always yearned for. The flow began, running through him, and it was everything. Immutable power surged and flowed through his being. It wrapped itself around the dying man. Again the coursing surge of light, again through the top of the man's head, again shattering the grey and illuminating the true Soul. The fellow looked up, and seemed to recognise him, seemed to know him.

Albert saw the fear fade from the man's eyes, as the incredible death came and took him from his body. So peaceful, this drowning. So wonderful, this experience. So blissful this sweet, sweet moment. Away the man went, leaving the disincarnate wreckage behind.

Another calling. A shot had rung out, a policeman had fallen with a bullet to his heart. The ebony black azure of power had left him, and the man's mortal being wavered until the moment Albert arrived. Seeing him, the officer knew it was time to go. The power flowed, the ecstasy renewed itself, the vapour formed, and the compassion took control. Such beauty, such complete and total embracement.

Every day, every hour, every minute, every moment another call came through. Albert now knew there would always be someone requiring his power, the power of freedom. All about were people in prison, longing to be free, and he held the keys.

Such a thing to be given. Such a small world to be awoken from, such a bottomless pit should Albert ever try to go back. He could not go back to what he was, not after knowing the exquisite taste of Lady Death upon his lips.

In a world transparent to the divine, Albert was now the bridge, the calling card for a new life. Or should he pass this cup? Was this really a curse? Should he just give the glasses to another? Could he? Would he?

As if in response, an empty yearning stood waiting. Somewhere in the distance, Leonard Cohen's "Bird on a Wire" was playing on a radio.

Silken, sweet Death awaits his answer. She is a most patient lady.

AWAKE AT FIVE O'CLOCK

Awake at Five O'clock, and the only thing that greeted Uri in the growing light of dawn was that revolting pile of papers, each one demanding payment for any of a hundred different bills. He had lost desire to file, respond, or even care about them. They had been tossed to that one spot as an avoidance, but they were insidious creatures. They started, and they stalked him, and accused him, and called him a failure. In his dreams they followed like a dark messenger of doom.

He massaged his face with cold water, shaking loose the horror that woke him as it always did. He washed his eyes in an effort to rub out the nightmare, but it would not leave. He still had the terrifying vision of the unseen enemy chasing him down empty streets in a cold dark city. Every corner was a choice between life or death, and every moment was a search for some safe haven. And awake, at ten minutes past five, the nightmare continued.

Twisted sheets, wrung with sweat, advertised his suffering. Uri looked back at the bed, but knew that getting back to sleep was just not an option. He braced for another pointless day which would stretch until he arrived back to another feverish night of tossing and turning, running from the demons.

Each night pursued by faceless men. Each night he must run until he came to the final corner, the last fatal decision. The one he could not risk and which kept waking him, night after night after night. And tomorrow he would be doing exactly this again, the ugly sound of leather slapping on the pavement behind him, driving him, wanting to devour him whole.

If not the demons of the night it was the bills of the morning. And there they were again, staring him down like some bull in the arena, looking at a naked fool. Bills do not speak, they whisper. They tell you what a fool you have been, what a waste of your opportunities you created, and all the time they laugh at your anxiety. Like a drugged singer in a seedy nightclub singing a torch song about the ending of a love, they sit silently, playing the death knell to your hopes and aspirations.

There they sit, mocking him, just like his wife used to. In his minds eye he saw when her tears had turned to rage, as those little pieces of paper piled up. and up. It was a barometer of sorts, as the depth of paper increased the accusations deepened, and the fury burned colder and more brittle in her eyes.

As the needle went from "Overdue" to "Pay up Now" to notes of "Pay Up or Else" to debt collectors calling in personally, threatening bankruptcy, she finally quit. She left him to his fate. She said it was because of the booze, but he knew it was the bills that pushed her out the door.

"If you didn't drink so much" she would cry, "then maybe we would stand a chance." She never realised this was simply not possible. Uri was an alcoholic, and he preferred his booze to her nagging, so why should he stop? Finally she left, and Uri just kept drinking. Only now he drank more, cursing the world and the whores that ran it more vehemently.

Bitterness ran so deep that it even poisoned the well of friendship. His artless commentary about the foibles of human nature that he saw in his friends was funny at first. But one by one, each in their turn were jabbed by the vitriol. So, as drinking buddies do when the party runs sour, they left him to it.

Uri simply drifted to drinking tables where mere poison was a virtue. In the world of alcoholic misery, all are strangers to themselves and each other, and it is best that such fellows remain on distant terms. From one bar to the next, and finally to his home in the early hours, Uri's life tumbled into an alternating succession of regrets and neglects. So it was that even as he became appalled by the immensity of his loneliness, he welcomed it. He pursued his misery like a Lemming pursues a cliff.

Uri woke up every morning, hating. He hated the world, he hated his friends, he hated the wife who left him and he hated his job. His Job! Tears welled up in the eyes as the last addition to the pile of bills glared at him.

TERMINATED: DUE TO … It didn't matter what the lie was that they supplied as a reason. Excuses were irrelevant. Not even the employer who he had worked for now for what, over 20 years, could tell him the truth. Uri hated him for this. It was the second in charge who had greeted him at the pay window when he went to collect his cheque. The man had nervously bridged the gap between them with the envelope marked "Uri Tyson: Notice to Quit"

At the time he laughed. The irony of the honesty of the envelope against the dishonest shuffling of a man he had been on nodding terms with for half his life struck him. All the bullshit struck home. Sharp focus fell on all the times he had prostrated his dignity to please some Hitler, the thousand little slights of some boss ignoring what he had to say, the million small put-downs, back-stabbings, and moral sapping lethargies that was part of his connection to this place.

All gone! It was GONE. The problem was removed. It with half relief, half anger and half sardonic wit that spoke as he said to his former workmate, "So then Bill, it is Bill isn't it? I mean, 20 years, and I think that's your name. I guess you are the lucky one, hey?"

Things were not so laughable now. No job, no friends, no savings and an ex-wife getting him evicted from his own house. He abused her solicitor over this, when he called to advise that the bailiffs would be there in 3 days. All he got was a click of the receiver and a short note saying further communication would be via letter only.

Today was that day. He ignored the filthy sheets and the smell from the pile of 2 month old washing. Dust had glued itself into every nook since his wife's departure, leaving behind this patina of regret. It was of no consequence. Compared to the enormity of the problems facing him, it was all nothing.

He was pleased that the rats had deserted the ship, because now he could do whatever he damn well wanted. No accusing eye if he pissed on the toilet seat at night, no bitter commentary as he fished a beer from the fridge. Yes, he was pleased despite the stress and angst. He was pleased to wilfully drown himself in his circumstances, because it showed he had some sense of ownership over the direction of his life, albeit one that it was ever downwards.

And this was the start of the homeless man.

He planned his exit carefully. He wanted the best return possible for the time left of this farce he called his life. His moment had come to laugh at all the bills while they stood there, helpless. Little pieces of paper driven to his door by even smaller minded men, who were run by callous bastards, who were owned by nasty large bankers, who worshipped these little pieces of paper.

He hated them all. He hated himself. He just hated. The small, endless wheel of meaningless habit, useless work and pointless existence was to be discarded this day, this very hour. He would embrace a new wheel, one that, as he tied himself to its rim, he knew would crush him to nothing. But he just didn't care.

The bailiffs arrived to find Uri cleaned up, clean shaven and wearing a suit and tie. He took just one small bag with the basics. Change of shirt, socks, toothbrush, etc. All new, bought from the supermarket last night. The rest was too dirty with the past to follow him to his new world. He walked from his house like a revived ghost.

Most men fear death, but not Uri. He welcomed it, desired it, embraced its python-like grip, as slowly but surely he intended to suck his last through the end of a bottle. He fully embraced the only friend he could trust, dear old alcohol. You always knew what to expect, what was happening, and where things were going, yet the insane unpredictability of this mad parade of Bacchus kept everything interesting.

Death should be like an expensive hooker, someone who you spend all night with, someone who teases, delights, distresses and distracts. Someone who costs you everything you have just for the pleasure of that moment to savour. You know what the result will be, but you spend as long as you can to avoid it in order to enjoy it more.

Awake at Five O'Clock: Part Two

Social Security paid little attention to Uri. As long as the formalities were complete and the bureaucratic process obeyed, then there was no further interest in another broken soul. There were too many passing through, and each was simply a statistic that reflected the downside to the cost of living.

Being a statistic was convenient, because you become invisible, and invisible people are free. You become coagulated with the other vast armada of invisible souls, who would be collected by the computer and presented in a small black folder to some politician, who could then parrot on about how much the State was doing for the downtrodden. You become someone else's problem, not your own.

Within any given bureaucracy, the failed percentage and the persona-non-gratis are one and the same. They are usually united by a nondescript manila folder, held by some faceless man who has carefully filed it in the annuls of time, until it all becomes forgotten. Uri, along with the rest of the failures, had become a thoroughly incongruous tribute to the power of society to grind you down to the lowest form of grit.

Such were Uri's thoughts as he stood in yet another endless line where the poor and sick and stupid and criminal and depraved were required to stand. He laughed. Finally he had made it to the Group W bench of Alice's Restaurant.

Regrets passed by like phantoms. Forgotten dreams would surface at odd times, like when, as a child, he dreamed of sailing. As an adult he bought a power boat, that broke down. Typical. First, he wanted to sail, but bought a power boat. Second, he was pissed it broke down, and: Third, he was annoyed that he sold off for half what it had cost him. Maybe he should have fixed it? Maybe gone fishing with his friends? There were no boats or friends now.

There was nothing but the booze. He was just another statistical failure in another queue, sitting with other failures who gritted down to peer into 5 year old magazines they didn't like to read. Why are there so many magazines about celebrities who didn't care about anyone or anything other than their celebrity? Then something snapped. Uri just looked at the rest of them there, sucking on cigarettes, looking bored, and laughed.

"You stupid C..nts!" Uri exploded with the comprehension of his reality. "Can't you see how f…ing funny this crap is? All mice on the f…ing treadmills, all of us. Those idiot ones behind the counter smug and secure, and here we are, pieces of sh..t pretending to be human. The people walking past pretending we don't f…ing exist. It's just so f…ing ridiculous.

"I used to think this pace was for bludgers. But now here I am. But we're not bludgers! We are failed f…ing GODS. Think about it people, we are f…king GODS. We don't do nothing, but we are given f…ing money by those minute fleas behind the counter! These people are our f…ing SERVANTS! Wake up! Have some respect! You are a f…ing GOD! And why? Because we all f…ing FAILED!"

His laughter at this irony filled up the empty space, while the clients cradled their magazines just a little tighter, not looking up. Just another mad drunk. However, Uri's name seemed to be called very quickly, and he was out the door with his first cheque in under an hour. Somewhat of a record.

He was still laughing outside, when it struck him. He had nowhere to go. He supposed he would have to find a boarding house somewhere, then it struck him that he had left the bottle opener at home. So after a few celebratory drinks while he declared his freedom to some other barflies, he wandered back to see if the bailiffs were done, only to find every single thing he had owned stuck into boxes and left on the footpath.

"F..K" he said. "That damn woman had already been there and TIDIED! Unbe-f..inglievable." He fished through, but no bottle opener. "Hey bitch queen!" he called out "You forgot the bottle opener!" In a few seconds it came flying through an open window and skewered the grass near his feet.

He looked immensely pleased with himself, and picked it up. Leaving everything else, he went back to the bar he had come from, and the room he had rented for that night. A week later, broke and retching from cheap wine, he was in the gutter making a closer acquaintance with Mr Death.

Time found Uri wandering from lodging to lodging, exchanging as little money as he could for increasing levels of crud, and lessening levels of respect. He discovered dankness at its best, land-ladies at their worst and hopelessness at its finest, as he moved from cheap to ever cheaper rooms. Finally he ended up camping in deserted warehouses on the waterfront.

Here he found permanent comfort. Here he found like-minded souls who had only one rule "Mind your own business". The law was obeyed to the letter, and it gave Uri some much needed security, and at last, some real friendship. When you finally fall to the very bottom of the well and look up, only then can you see the stars. And with the rent so easily looked after, here on the lowest rung there was no shortage of drink.

This was a world where you were judged by your stories. Who you were, where you came from, these meant nothing. How you told a joke, and how you entertained: This was what made you a King. And but damn it, Uri was a funny bastard when he got going. Here he found people who loved him for what he was, which granted, wasn't much, but at last it was enough. It was enough.

Death could come here and find him smiling. He even gave their deserted warehouse a name "MYOFB" – Mind Your Own F...king Business.

"Thou shalt not give a f...k about thy neighbours problem, unless it lessens the depth of your bottle" he had written on the wall with a red crayon he had found in a dumpster. On another he had written "When your back is against the wall, turn around and write on the f...ker". Hey, it was stupid, but some photographer from the Times had been down to take photos, and placed Uri as the author, squarely in one of them.

After it was published, the journalist even brought Uri down the copy, which showed him with his mates, laughing, on the front cover. The title read: "Never so down and out that laughter and wit can't shine"

No wonder they loved Uri. He made them all stars.

The camaraderie and good times had their ups and downs, of course. Occasionally some yahoo's in a car with furry dice hanging from the rear-vision mirror would come to have fun kicking the drunks, but the smart ones knew when it was Friday or Saturday night, and they were out of sight. Overall, it was a pretty good life, and there were no bills, no nagging wives, and no "pissing up the pants of your boss to keep your job" people about.

Then one night, as Uri and his friends stood around a 44 gallon drum they had been made into a temporary furnace, some fellow called out his name. A man in a suit had gotten out of an expensive car, and called out for him at random. "Uri Tyson! I am looking for Uri Tyson!"

Uri was going to ignore it, obviously just some suit who had some legal crap he didn't need, but maybe it was something to do with his social security cheque? "Yeah ?" he answered. "What you want?"

The man handed him a letter, saying it was from his former wife, and could he please read it, sign it, and hand it back. "well f...k you friend, thanks for the kindness." Uri replied. Then the "friend" held up a $100 bill, and said that after signing the documents it would be his, His friends cheered, so Uri obliged. He opened the letter up, and read out aloud so all could hear:

Dear Uri.

After all this time I find the pain we have gone through has eased. I am now living at a new address, have a new life, and am now able to leave the past behind. I trust you have done so as well. Forgive me that I do not pass on the new details of my life, but I have found another man who loves me and I do not want to drag the past along behind me. I hope you will understand. He wishes to marry me, thus the reason for this note.

I saw your article in the Times, and a friend recognised the place, so I have sent a legal fellow down to find you. As you may have guessed, this letter is about finalizing the divorce. There is paper work that was not signed before you left, and it must be done if we are to finish this matter.

The other main point is that I have sold the house, and in doing so have discharged all debts that were in your name. Since it was decided there was to be a 50/50 split in all revenue coming from the sale of marital property, I have deducted these costs from your settlement. I do hope you will not be too disappointed, but considering the circumstances I would imagine you are simply pleased to be free of the concern.

A cheque for the residual is enclosed, along with a proper inventory of costs. You will note also the final Divorce Papers that need to be signed. Sorry, but I have made the cashing of this cheque conditional on these papers being filled in and returned to the man who gave you this letter.

It would have been nice to have a happy ending, but we are not living in a fairy tale.

Goodbye Uri ... I do wish you the best.

Sincerely
Eva

Uri looked at the cheque. Three Thousand, Two Hundred and Fifty Four Dollars. $3254 for a lifetime of work, while the bitch painted her nails, and complained about everything. Bitterness swelled up and he threw the divorce papers into the furnace, a final act to show the cow what he thought.

Yet as he did so, time stopped, and a strange sensation came over him. The fire started twisting around the paper, wanting to devour it, holding it suspended inside a voracious beast. Time stopped, then it started to reverse. Uri's whole life unwound before him. All the pain that had been driven into his bones, every lick of insult he had ever suffered, every insignificant look he had ever received all flooded back in that instant.

It was like a really bad "B" grade movie. And then the dream came again. Once more he was being chased down dark alleys, finding blind corners and an agony of indecision as to what to do next. How could he escape to freedom?

Down twisting corridors he ran, mindlessly hunting for a solution. Futility boiled in his veins, dried out his mouth, and fear took over his heart. But the ancient desperate will to survive took over and he kept running, and running until it felt his heart would burst.

The flames reached higher, licking against his brain like the dry thirst that plagued him, but then it changed! In the midst of the agony he BECAME the fire. It took him completely, and he became it. The flames no longer burned. The fear no longer controlled him. Then he realised THIS was the final corner, the final decision, the final choice to be free or to die.

Silent, invisible tears rolled down his face as he came back to this world, watching the fire consume the last of the divorce papers and thinking "F…k me, $3254 will buy a lot of booze!"

"Ah, sorry about that. Impulse." He said to the lawyer who was still standing there. "How do I go about cashing the cheque now?"

The lawyer pulled out another envelope, saying "I brought a spare"

Opening it up, and taking the extra $100 that had been offered, Uri signed where the little red arrows told him to. He laughed, he laughed so hard. All his life had come down to $3254. It was the greatest joke in all of history, and now, finally Uri could see it. In the middle of signing, laughing, he said to his friends "Yes friends, you too can invest your whole existence into a lie, and, when you do, an enormous reward will be handed to you on a platter by some nice gentleman in a suit and tie."

Everyone but the lawyer laughed. Uri was just so damn funny, and no doubt he would have another story to tell this evening.

"My wife wants a divorce!" he said. "Can you believe it? She doesn't want to stay married to me. What you reckon, should I give it to her?"

"Sh..t yeah," came the dry reply from everyone. "Otherwise she might want to come down here looking for you, and what would the f…king neighbours think then! She would lower the tone of the whole place."

Laughter and good times and much drinking went long into the night.

Authors Note: Uri died shortly after he told me his story. He was a drunk on the streets of Woolloomooloo, Sydney. He had been a solicitor, but felt his life was a lie, until he became an alcoholic. He said that for the first time in his life, he felt honest. To put this in perspective, he was raised in an upper middle class suburb in Melbourne, wealthy parents, excellent education. Everything everyone wants for their children. It didn't work for him.

At that point, he had just shifted to Metholated Spirits.

I asked if he understood what this meant, and he knew. He figured he had six months max. I asked why, and he simply said that after a while the alcohol no longer worked, but the meth did.

He was prepared to pay the cost, and kept right on smiling as he beat me in yet another game of chess. I miss him.

Thank you to Mr Diogenes

A long, long time ago there was a Greek Philosopher

His words touched the heart of the Alexander the Great

The King had travelled far to meet the philosopher, this Diogenes

And he offered the man anything he could wish for.

> The philosopher had been asleep in a yard when the great king called
>
> And appeared to sleep soundly still
>
> But was prodded by his students, who told him of the great offer
>
> Diogenes looked at the king, and said "I can have: Anything?"

The King said, ANYTHING

The philosopher asked that the King step to one side

Because he was blocking his sun

And interrupting his sleep

> That's why I say Thank You to Mr Diogenes

Just Rubbish

I have to say, Robert looked odd as he dropped over the TV. He owed me some money, and giving me this in lieu of cash. I didn't really want it, as I never really watched the idiot box, especially an old black and white like this. But it meant he felt less obligated, and he was a friend.

He had walked in just as I had been reading the obituaries, which was one of my curious habits that I dabbled in of a Saturday morning in Sydney. The obituaries came after the marriages, where I loved trying to pick the faces of people that would stay together. Some people just share features, and you feel they will last, while others look like strange birds, each from a different species.

I read a really odd obituary out to Rob. And there was a tag-line to an article. Apparently some fellow down in Elizabeth Bay has passed away, and he was dead for 3 weeks before anyone noticed. *Man, that's what I call lonely*, I had thought to myself. His whole place was a complete jumble of crap. Every room was full of junk that looked as if it had been pulled in from the council clean up piles. The only free space in the whole house was in a bedroom, that was frozen in the 1960's and where no one had slept for years, and in the kitchen, where the old man was found dead, slumped over a cup of cold tea. He had a camp bed in there, so I guessed he had crowded his life into that corner.

Robert said nothing for a while, then he said "I can't give you this TV. It's from that guy's house. Wouldn't be right."

"What? Did you steal it?"

"Nah, but some kids that owed me money did, which was the money I owed to you. They gave me the box. But I can't pass on a curse, hey?"

I was interested, and not knowing the story, asked what had happened. And I warn you: This is possibly the saddest story I had ever been told.

Rob had been putting up with a couple of smack addicts who had been camping at his place. They came back a little while ago with the TV he now had, saying "Here, we owe you some money, so take this. But hey, we have just seen the most incredible place. You have to come check it out."

Rob went with them down the road to one of the last of the wooden houses in Elizabeth Bay. The paint was falling off, the garden overgrown, and the lawn had not been looked at in years. It was a remnant of a Sydney long past, an echo of the 1940's that survived to the present day (1986). "Come in, you won't believe it!" Tom said, with no concept of what others called private property.

Up the back stairs they went, the door was unlocked, or more to the point, Rob could see where they had forced it open. The place seemed deserted, but it stank of old man and dust and loneliness. They went into the back room, a sunroom of sorts which was his kitchen, living room and bedroom. Rob saw the outline in the dust where the TV had just been and started to say something. But Tom and Jed were already past him and into the rest of the house.

"Have a gander at this unbelievable crap!" Through into a darkened room they went, Rob followed. It was remarkable, because against every wall there were rows and rows of neatly stacked boxes that seemed full of stuff. The boxes were piled on top of each other like precarious totem poles, each having its own point of balance, and each covered in layers of dust, untouched in an age. The lounge was full with row upon row of boxes, erected like a huge domino field, each one full of whatever. In the 5 x 5 meter lounge room there was only a walking space between the box rows, of which Rob counted nine, each running the full length of the room. Organised madness.

The curtains had faded and were falling apart with age, but in the sad light they showed an incredible world of hoarding, isolated within one small house. Outside they were surrounded by a sea of humanity and high-rise apartments, yet here everything was a time capsule. Each room was the same, rows upon rows of boxes, with the exception of the main bedroom. There a queen-size bed sat with a lace overthrow covering it, and in the middle, a framed photo frame holding a picture of what must have been the man's wife.

They moved back out to the corridor. "Ubef..kinglievable, hey?" said Tom. Then he reached up, and pulled down a box. "Wonder what sort of sh..t is in these." Of course, taking one down to look meant a few others came with it. Dust spewed up and they had to leave that spot, sneezing and coughing. When it settled they peered back in, and all there was scattered on the floor were odd bits of things that other people had apparently tossed out. Stupid things, in no particular order and serving no purpose at all. A doll without a head, a threadbare stuffed toy, a photo frame with broken glass.

Jed spoke up, "What an old c..nt! What a f..king waste of a f..king life, and a waste of our f..king time. Let's piss off." And as he turned around, he kicked over a pile of boxes, knocking them to the floor. Then, for no particular reason, he picked up a cricket bat that had fallen out, went into the bedroom, and smashed the photo of the woman.

Then the thing happened. The animal inside took over the boys, and they started rampaging through the place, knocking everything over, coughing and laughing as the dust and mildew of the ages became a storm of irritation. Rob headed out the back door, stopping only to see the photo beside the empty space where the TV had been. It was another one of the guys wife. He saw no photos of kids or any other family, just the wife. "Poor bastard" he said to himself.

Tom called out, and came into the back room with the cricket bat. "Hey look at this!" he shouted, and started smashing into the boxes, scattering rubbish everywhere. Then he saw the photo, and with no thought to the contrary, smashed it.

That was enough for my friend, he left them to it, and headed back home.

Years ago Rob had told me of a Federation house he and some friends had found in the back country of South Australia. It was a beautiful home, stone walls, cedar panelling, marble fireplaces. And it had been abandoned. He camped in there for months, got the stove working, fixed the water tanks and slowly friends from up North heard of the hang-out pad, and had arrived on their bikes. For a time it was great.

They grew some hooch, spent their dole money on booze, and partied all night. Then one evening something happened, something just like that poor bastards house he was just leaving. Some pigs got it into their head to pull down the cedar panels and burn them. It was cold, it was winter, but the Cedar was soon gone so they ripped up everything they could. And when it was all done, they got pissed off and started attacking the fireplace, pulling up floorboards, and smashing the windows.

The house took 48 hours to be completely ruined, so then they put a match to it. He had asked me years ago why people do this, and even to this day I don't know. The animal just runs riot. "Sounds like the South Australian house all over again, but different, hey?"

Rob just nodded. He didn't look happy.

I showed him the photo in the Sydney Morning Herald. "Yeah," he said "That's the place. What happened?"

"No one knows. The old guy was found the other day in the back room, slumped over the table where the TV had been, holding the smashed photo of his dead wife. No known cause of death. Looks like he just sat there and died. Police asked questions, and apparently the wife had passed on some 30 years ago and he had been on his own ever since.

"He never spoke to anyone, kept to himself, and no one in the street even knew his name. He was only discovered because the power meter guy smelled the dead body and saw the open door. Poor bastard." I said

Rob didn't say anything. He just took the TV and left. I heard him tossing it into the trash downstairs as he made his way out. He never mentioned it again, and up till the writing of this story, I had never thought to remind him.

LADDER TO THE MOON

"The youth gets together his materials to build a ladder to the moon, and, at length, the middle-aged man concludes to build a woodshed with them."

Thoreau

It was time to make the journey. It was time to take the girl up to the cabin by the lake, the old shack his father had owned, and his father before him. Now HE was the old man, creaking each morning, waiting for the sun to warm his bones, and it was time to pass on the message, and hope that this one might catch it. So that someone might carry on with the torch.

Near his death, so many years ago now, his father had called him over to give his son some final words, and in his hand were the title deeds. He said, "Son, this place is a jewel. A jewel that has no value to anyone, but it is worth everything to me because I love it. This place is priceless because no money could buy it from me, but I want to give it away to someone who will come to love it like I do.

"The other boys are good men at heart, but you, you always had that distant look. This is the right place for you. I just ask you one thing before I go. Keep this shack in your heart, and keep it in the family. If you do, it will always help you and those you love. It will help you remember what is important in life."

And so too, down the years, it was now his time. He could hear it calling, the other worlds. Time to make that final journey, his bones told him. So with this in mind he went with the grandchild into the wilderness, no longer the strapping youth, or the caring father. He was just the old man, the Grandfather.

But he still had value, like that old shack. He knew things, he saw thing others didn't, and he wanted to show this favoured child something that was not

TV, or video games, something that had nothing to do with fashion or fancy things. He wanted to show her the simplicity of nature. So he took her to his secret place, the place that made HIS childhood special. Up, away, high up in the hills, miles from the city they went.

The last leg was a walk in of several miles, and after a couple of hours they came to the old cabin. No one had visited in a while, so together they spent the day brushing out the dust and cobwebs, and bringing in the wood for the fire. Night came, and it was full moon. The girl saw it shining on the lake, and gasped at the beauty. "It is like a ladder on the lake, Grandpa, a Ladder to the Moon!"

The Grandfather smiled, and laughed softly. His face, washed with wrinkles, became young again and he asked with a smile, now knowing what he had to say to the girl. "That Ladder you see, what happens when you touch it?"

"It is just the reflection on the water, you know that Gramps" she answered, smiling.

"But the Moon is still there, isn't it?" he asked.

"Of course it is. The Moon is there forever!" She laughed.

The old man stopped, looked at the little one, and said quite seriously. "That's right little one. The Moon IS there forever, but the Ladder to the Moon, it's just a reflection on a lake. You can't climb it, you cannot touch it, but yet there it is anyway."

"It's a pretty ladder," the girl spoke up, "And look! A duck is up late and splashing in it!"

Soon the water settled, and the shimmering path of light resumed its silent witness.

"This Ladder to the Moon that you see. It is like your dreams, your hopes and your wishes. These are fragile things, and they will break if you touch them with doubt or suspicion. This Ladder is defenceless. Anyone can beat it, win against it, defeat it with just a brush of their hand. Even a Duck up late can disturb it! (she laughs) Yet no one can defeat it forever. You see how the light will always return, and always point to the moon? (the girl nods) No matter what you do, it will return, and it will always point to the moon. Remember this about your deepest dreams. No matter how difficult life becomes, always remember that when your heart is stilled, all your dreams will return and point towards something that is eternal."

The young girl seemed a little puzzled, so the old man explained further.

"Our dreams are not forever. Today you wished for an ice cream, but tomorrow it will be a new doll. That's OK. Our dreams change like the reflection on the water, here today, gone tomorrow. But inside, deeper inside, is a great dream, a good dream, a dream of higher things which will lead us to things that DO last. This is that part which is the REAL you, the spark of life inside. The part of you that seeks only good, and which fears no evil.

"And when you find this, you discover something even more important. When you understand the value of your own dreams and wishes, you learn to appreciate the dreams and wishes of another. Then you can allow others to have the freedom to choose their path. Then your heart, begins to shine. It becomes something unshakable inside you, even though all the storms would blow and the earth itself would move.

"If you can become someone who considers that another's dreams and goals are ALSO precious things, not to be touched or ignored or doubted, then you will have discovered the greatest secret of all. That the Moon is not up in the sky, it is inside your heart.

"So little one, tell me: What is your dream?"

"Just to stay here a little longer." the little girl answers, not really understanding the words, but feeling the love. Somehow she knew Gramps was saying goodbye.

The Grandfather looked into her eyes, and saw the reflection of the moon on a small tear that welled up on the rim. He said nothing as it grew, and fell. He listened as the little one sobbed and ran into his arms. He felt her heart feel the moment, and he said nothing, but his thoughts ran down an entire lifetime.

Right here is his safe place. This is where he came throughout his life when times were hard. When he was in Europe fighting a war, he came here in his thoughts. When his wife died, he came here. When his son killed himself in a car accident, he came here. When his own children failed to understand him, he came here. This was his spiritual home. Places like this, he thought to himself, are important for the Soul. Places like this are where Soul can emerge and shine freely, like the Full Moon in the sky.

Here you can come and watch the reflection of your thoughts and your feelings play out on the backdrop of nature. Here you can pause, and cut from the ways of the world, and just be yourself. He thought long and deep, and as he sat looking out to the world beyond, she fell asleep in his arms. "If we have to fight for something in life, little one, it should be for places like this, and times like these." He murmured as he scooped her up and put the little girl to bed.

"Thank you for showing me the Moon, and her ladder, Grandpa." she whispered as he drew the covers over her. The old man smiled, and thought about the world and all the changes he had seen. He thought back to his own father, and his grandfather who had bought this place so long ago. And of course, they were here, watching. They were like his dreams, part of the play of light and shadow that pointed to the moon. Soon he would be with them again.

Finally, after all these years, maybe he had found the one he could leave it to. "So few cherish anything of real value anymore." he said to his father, and his grandfather, and to the shadows on the wall, and to the spirits of the Lake, and the whispering soul of the wood. "So few cherish themselves."

He laughed. The irony of his death becoming the gift of life to another tickled something deep inside. The old man, putting on his bi-focals, sat to write. "I, John Alexander Thornton, being of sound mind and body…"

GILBERT

Gilbert was an odd fellow. I liked him a lot, and I was never sure why. He had a gawky, angular face, brown eyes that loped off to the horizon at every opportunity, and a sense of being uncomfortable wherever he went. His long cheeks seemed slightly hollow, and framed by brown hair that was permanently uncombed. Most of all, he had this huge smile, with large, white teeth behind it.

There was no reason for it, but you just liked him. Everyone liked Gilbert, even when they didn't! He was just so agreeable, friendly, and happy. It is hard to dislike anyone who does not hold a view that opposes your own, which is not to say he was a jellyfish. Far from it, Gilbert simply considered deeply any thought you might care to voice. A notion would come his way, and he would cock his head to one side, eyes trailing out into the concept, and he would see whatever he could see from your side of the fence. Then you would then see him hopping onto the other side of that fence, to see how it looked from there.

Some people thought he was a little simple. Simple? I was never so certain, though he appeared that way. He certainly didn't appear complicated. Yet often he came out with some really curious observations that were right on the money, so idiot savant simple, maybe, but just simple, no.

He liked to soak himself in other people's views. Indeed, he had walked so many miles in so many people's moccasins that I am not sure if he knew where his own shoes were anymore. Perhaps it was a lack of self, rather than any lack of intelligence, that got people thinking he was a little odd? Whatever it was that drove Gilbert, there was no unkindness or malice behind any of it.

It appeared to me that he lived at Martine and Pedro's place, but apparently he was always just visiting. He had mentioned he had a flat nearby, but as he lived on his own, and as Martine and Pedro seemed to like him, well. We go where we are loved. He spent a lot of time there. And that proved he wasn't stupid, because Martine was a great cook.

As it turned out, on this day when I was visiting her with a few $2 bottles of red, Gilbert was there and feeling quite unusually talkative. Perhaps it was the wine. We downed the first bottle, and then I found another, and finally Gilbert started to loosen up, and actually chat about himself.

As it turned out, for the last 6 months he had been working a job in the city, in the public service. Now, Gilbert was a poet, and definitely not a bureaucrat. I could not believe he could get such a job, let alone survive in it. Yet this is exactly what had transpired. Talk about square pegs and round holes.

Obviously, his peculiar mannerisms and the way he listened intently to everyone drew the attention of his superior, who formed a fairly swift opinion that there was something wrong with the young man. He was sent for drug testing, which he would have failed dismally except for the fact that a fellow worker had smuggled him a clean urine sample, that he subsequently provided to the good doctors.

Having cleared the drug hurdle, he was then sent for psychoanalysis. This naturally became the main topic of our conversation, especially as we headed for the third bottle of vino. "A Pysche? What were you seeing a psyche for?"

"Well," said Gilbert in his perfect dead-pan delivery, "that was exactly why I was seeing a psyche! To see if I needed to see one."

"That's crazy." Martine added, returning to us briefly from the planet she had been visiting. Her dreams called her away once more soon after. Martine was the original flower child, gorgeous auburn hair, blue eyes, clear heart. A truly beautiful girl who, barely a year after this conversation took place, did a Ken Keyes course, and decided she needed more money. She flipped from hippie flower child to a short haired, highly paid, finance professional.

At the same time, her boyfriend Pedro, who worked on the railways and was as straight as a die ALSO flipped. During that same year later he dumped his job, smoked copious amounts of hooch, grew his hair into dreadlocks, and became a peace activist. Weird how things move in the shifting tides of life.

But not Gilbert. He was a constant. He was an immovable person of dreams who sailed through life on a whisper of contentment. So the idea of him having to face up to a psychiatrist was a difficult thing to fathom. However, he was paid to go, and it took up every Friday morning for some 4 months. This day had apparently been his final appointment, and he was to find out in the coming week if he had passed, and thus sane and employed, or otherwise, and fired.

"I have bills, you know" he said. I had gathered that this was a possibility. "And I have rent to pay. I am feeling very stressed with all of this."

I asked him to tell us more. "Why," I queried, "Why did they see fit to send you to a Psyche in the first place?"

"It's complicated, or more to the point, where I work is full of complicated people. Apparently because I talk and listen but don't wear clothes like they do, I am suspect. I do understand that some people do not like me, and I accept this. I don't know why they can't accept me, though. It makes me feel very uncomfortable." He said.

I had to agree that, given his situation, I too would have felt uncomfortable. "Have you ever considered that it is not you, but the people you work with that have the problem?"

"Oh indeed I do. I tried to point out this very possibility to the psychiatrist on my second or third visit, but all he did was nod knowingly and write a whole lot of stuff down. In fact, that was all the fellow ever seemed to do. But that's not the half of it. He has this really thick German accent, as well as a picture of Sigmund Freud on the wall. I felt uncomfortable with this as well, but of course I didn't say anything about that to him at the time."

"Why not?" I asked.

"Well, I don't think he liked me, so I decided to say as little as possible. That's when he started asking me about my mother and father and what happened with my brothers and sisters, and if I had a pet. All of those sorts of questions."

"What did you tell him?"

"Well, I am an orphan, raised by an elderly aunt. What was there to tell? I fed the dog next door. That's about it really. My childhood was simply a waiting room, which is why I took up poetry, to fill in the time. He then wanted to read my poems, so I brought him in a few."

He showed me one of his Haiku, which went "Waiting, While the Wheels Smile, as they grind behind the desk." and a few other short, simple pieces. "Oh," I said, "I really don't think you should have shown THAT one to a Psychiatrist."

"Why not?" said Gilbert. "I wrote it about him after all."

"Let's not go there. What was his reaction? I mean, that poem is pretty in his face and basically saying that the guys just thinks too much."

"Oh yes! He wrote sheets of paper about it," Gilbert said, laughing. "In fact the whole of this session he called a breakthrough, and he wrote copious notes for the entire 2 hours I was there. I am sure he thought the poems were about myself. He asked me odd question as he read them, and I offered a few words, and he wrote and wrote and wrote. Finally I said to him that he was writing 50 times more than I was speaking, and you know what he answered?"

"No … tell me."

"He said 'It's what you DON'T say that counts!' and he said it with an air of triumph, as if he had cracked the code at last."

We laughed till we fell off the chair. When you are nearing the end of the third bottle things can become hysterically funny. I could see it: the thick German accent, the short thick spectacles, and badly fitting cheap suit. The perfect picture of some public service failure with a degree who was looking for a way to justify his existence.

"Well, that was the last visit before today's, and today I am not sure if it went so well. You see, now he started to get to questions of how I dressed and WHY I dressed the way I did. I have to say, I was getting pissed off because he was just being nosy."

"What did he ask about?" I asked, curious now as to the next stage of the matter.

"Well, I had on this Orange Shirt and these Green pants that you see." (I did see, it looked perfectly Gilbert-esque I thought) "Well, he pulled out notes from every day of every visit I had made, and he described the types of clothes I wore on each occasion, but then he came to the green pants and orange shirt, saying 'You have never worn this colour combination before. Why have you decided to wear this today?' Truly this is what he asked, so I decided to tell him the truth, but slowly.

"I looked from side to side as if there were a great secret, and drew him in. I asked 'Do you REALLY want to know, I mean REALLY?' The guy got excited, he could barely contain himself as he said "yes yes yes, I really want to know. I really do!' So I told him the truth.

"I said 'Well, I woke up (he was writing frantically) and I looked in the closet and I said to myself that I had to pick some clothes. Why? Because I had to go to WORK! (He writes more) At first I was going to wear blue jeans, but they needed a wash. I thought of the white shirt, but it was still wet and on the line. I then thought, maybe the 1970's body shirt, but it had been ripped by the last wash and was no good for work anymore.'

"The man was writing like he had never written before. He was like the hound on its scent, pursuing the quarry. So then I let it drop! 'That was when I looked into the wardrobe and saw the GREEN pants, and the ORANGE shirt and I thought PERFECT! That's PERFECT!'

"The fellow as beyond himself with excitement. He cried out 'And WHY was this perfect? WHY!' So I said 'Because they were the only clean things in my wardrobe.' And that was it. I stopped, and smiled. The man paled, swallowed deeply, shook his head and told me to get out of there."

I was laughing hard. I never knew Gilbert was a comedian, and I suspect that neither did he. But I could tell he was quite proud of himself. "What will you do if they fire you?"

"Oh, I don't know. Go back on the dole, I guess. I doubt if anyone else would hire me. Despite the strange people, the public service is a good place for me because all I have to do is sit at a desk and fill out forms, and do the other things they shove my way. Then it is all about just keeping up polite conversation with people around me. I can do that, you know."

Dear Gilbert. So innocent and so wise, all at the same time. You know, right up to that point I used to think he was a bit slow, but in that moment I realised he just worked on life from a different direction. He caught breezes that sailed to ports unknown, and had a certain tact that caught you by surprise.

"But really, when you think about it," I said "There IS some deep sort of reason why you bought the orange shirt and green pants in the first place. I mean, the green suits you, but the orange just isn't right on your skin. Do you think there may be a reason why you chose the orange in the first place?"

Gilbert looked from side to side, leaned forward, and whispered to me. "You know, there really IS a reason why I bought the orange shirt in the first place. You want to know?"

"Sure," I said "Give me the story."

"Well," he leaned forward conspiratorially and whispered, "I was walking past an Op Shop, and there it was! The last shirt in the 10 cent pile."

I could feel my leg getting mightily pulled. Martine was giggling beyond redemption, the wine was all gone, and Gilbert! Dear Sweet Gilbert! He had finally shown me his wicked side. I looked at him somewhat askance, and thought "And people think he is a little simple? Simply lethal, more like it."

You know, he wasn't fired. More to the point, his case was taken up by his union as a perfect example of management harassment. He was subsequently given a job at what was the perfect place for one with his nature, the Arts Council. He is probably there to this very day. His job is to listen to an artist's concept for a performance, and to recommend they be given grants if they seemed worthy.

Wonderful. He was so good at listening, and appreciating another view.

So, despite all appearance, Gilbert made a success of his life. And so I write this story for you, as a warning.

Should you be like so many others, and deem that a boy with a huge toothy smile, wearing an orange shirt and green pants is somewhat odd. Well, aren't we all? But more to the point, if you are not just a little bit odd, if YOU are not a little bit different, then maybe there is a problem YOU are not addressing?

Yes?

FALSI

There was a small cadre of expatriates from the human race who had gathered in a run down old office block in Pitt Street, Sydney. The dear lady, Hazel, who ran it for the man who owned the property (along with 1/4 of the rest of the Sydney CBD) knew we were living there, but she understood that it helped to stop the place getting broken into, and she turned a blind eye.

I had a couple of rooms, where I would write, and beside me my friend had a recording studio. We would do the odd project, package the odd would-be entertainer, and generally do whatever might earn a crust. I organized the now infamous Caves Concert from there, which introduced us to some of the glitterati of Australian Media.

Like any good play, there is always a wonderful cast of characters that circulate around the tale, and they are deserving of mention. There was Bill, the Tarot Card reader, who had left the Rajneesh people after experiencing the cruelty Montana, but who still wanted lots of sex. So he read Tarot Cards, not because he was psychic, but because women liked to have sex with men who did this sort of thing. At that point in time he had 36 girlfriends, and considered it far too stressful, and was contemplating giving up on the business.

The seamstress on the second floor was an enigmatic creature. Stunning, in her own way, and very regal. She made the most amazing leather coats, and the one I wanted, which she had up on the wall, was not for sale. "Why?" I asked. "It's a design for a movie," she replied, "one that will be made here. I am under contract and cannot make any replicas." That movie was "The Matrix" and if you thought the leathers look good on screen, in real life they were amazing.

Boo, an elfin creature of great inner beauty, lived immediately under me, and she was a performance sculptor artist. She had discovered a Mime act that made her a fortune: She dressed up in traditional Marcel Marceau white, with white makeup, red lips and cheeks, and a hat. Her act was extraordinary. She pushed this pram made from wire, which held a full size baby inside, also made entirely of wire. Yet it came alive when she held it.

All she would do was sit at street corners, look pathetic, and cradle her wire baby. Quite unbelievably, people threw money into her pram, and quite a lot of it, from what I could see. What this meant was that she had plenty of smoke and wine for visitors, therefore she had many visitors.

Falsi was an almost live-in regular. He was a curious fellow who often camped downstairs with Boo, and whose main claim to fame being that he was a genuine Bedouin. He spoke perfect English and was extremely white, but he explained that his father had sent him to Oxford, and that the Bedouin were all naturally white. He claimed his race were the "white negro" and told me that he could stand in the sun all day, completely naked, and he would never burn.

Well, it was a great story, and he was great fun.

For a period of over three months we three, Boo, Falsi and myself, often ended up in coffee shops in and around Kings Cross, talking and laughing until the early hours. Falsi always held center stage, and his stories were something else. They rode over you like a tide, and despite your belief that they may have been entirely fictitious, you were like King Canute to try and resist him, the tide of his tales had their way.

There was no separating Falsi from his stories, nor was there any shortage of them. They were incredible yarns of impossible things in improbable places. He was a walking, talking Hollywood script.

Yet I cannot recall a single detail! Not one single story he told remains in my thoughts. It was as if you were washed in them, then the bath water was drained so that the next night you could wash yourself all over again.

Finally, after some months I had a moment alone with him. He was sitting in his favorite Kings Cross café, the Piccolo Bar, talking quietly with the manager,

Vittorio, who had been a permanent fixture of the place for some 30 years. They both indicated for me to have a seat. Vittorio went, as always, to clean cups, and prepare coffee, so finally I was alone with the storyteller. That was when I asked him about the truth.

"Falsi, I love the stories. I am a writer, so I appreciate them more than most. But I am curious, how much of the story you tell us is true, and how much is to entertain?"

He looked at me with daggers. I felt extraordinarily uncomfortable, and for a few moments he just sat there, looking. Finally he spoke, "You understand nothing. In my country, such a question could have your throat cut. You are calling me a liar!"

"Not at all! " I stammered. "No, I was just curious because, as a writer, I am always having to find the balance between the truth and the dream."

He stopped, looked into the distance, and spoke: "You know, when I was a child my father would tell us stories every night. Each night I would fall asleep in the wonderful embrace of his deeds, feeling secure, rich and loved.

"He would have people come by our oasis, and stop at our tent, and all he would ask of them was what tales that had for him of the outside world. And if their tales were good, they were invited to stay with the family for as long as they wished.

"When you are in the desert, when the sum total of your life can be added up as camels, brothers and sisters, your mother and your father, your stories become what set you apart. Your stories are your wealth. The only thing of importance to you are the stories. They are everything. They are your sun at night, your blanket in winter, your water, your food and your lover.

"Now imagine if a man came to visit our oasis, and my father asked him of his journey in the outside world, and the man says 'Well I breathed 1234 times. My camel drank 3 pints of water. I wore out a pair of shorts. I prayed to Mecca 5 times every day. I saw a bird flying.' What would you think of such a man?

Without needing me to answer, he said, "You would think him a fool, yes?"

Indeed, when put like that, this is exactly what you would think.

"So what you are wanting to know is how many pairs of shorts were worn out in the making of this story? Is that it?" He looked at me as if I were three inches tall.

"When you are under a blanket of stars with no one else, all alone, the stories of life tell themselves to you. When finally you meet another Soul, your heart yearns to spread the wisdom of what you have discovered and the joy you found on your journey. The story is but the bridge for the LOVE you have to share. So why do you want to destroy the bridge? Do you feel you must show the man all the bricks you used to build it? Walk over it, and it is truth. Pull it apart, and it is a lie.

"You say you are a writer? I say that until all stories are truth, and until all stories are lies, then you do not understand the first thing about living. You are simply a recorder of letters. These things are simple. But when you learn REAL truth, you understand one clear reality: Friendship is more important than so-called truth. Understanding is more important than reality. Life is better than death. And the greatest of all secrets! We are alone, but we need not be lonely."

I felt chastised and vaguely stupid. For a moment the storyteller had become a hardened man of the world, someone who could quite easily cut your throat, if needs be, and what's more, the Bedouin could see that I saw this. Falsi just grunted, and said he had an appointment.

For a time I was not sure what had just happened. I had thought I was being friendly. I had believed I was speaking to someone I knew. Yet now he seemed such a total stranger, isolated, alone. Like myself, in other words.

I never saw him again. Those words were the last he spoke to me, and they are burned in my heart. They are the only thing I can remember of our time together. Three months I had spent with Falsi, and not a single story remained, then I realized: True stories, the ones that matter, are like clouds that give you everything, their total being, their essence, and once spent, they vanish.

I realized after he walked out that he had left open the book he was reading before I came in. On the table was Nicholson's translation of Rumi, opened at his famous "Song of the Reed"

> *Hearken to this Reed forlorn,*
> *Breathing, even since 'twas torn*
> *From its rushy bed, a strain*
> *Of impassioned love and pain.*

To this day, I honestly do not know if he was a spiritual master, or a fraud living off the good graces of Boo, the mime. Maybe both? Perhaps Falsi was not even a Bedouin. Perhaps his stories were all lies. Perhaps he was just some traveler entertaining himself by entertaining others. Yet perhaps he was a master storyteller, who had stopped by to teach me about everything that was important, by trying to get me to forget the rest.

I don't know.

I really have no idea, but I feel free when I think of him. And THIS, dear reader, this is the truth and the wonder of it all.

Bill – Tarot Card Reader

Most, including Bill himself, would admit that the craggy, worn face was not necessarily a thing of beauty, yet Bill never had a shortage of girlfriends. He had a very unique and powerful character, which is another way to say: ugly, but interesting. The doleful, red rimmed eyes, that gazed with general cynicism at anything other than a young girl, had seen much of life through the telescope of an empty bottle, and it showed in the rest of him.

You might be generous and say his features were well used. We had a variety of discussions on a number of subjects, specifically the lack of a bidet in the cheap rooms we rented, called offices on our rental contract, but at $45 a week, they were also cheap rent. As we shared the bathroom on the third floor, which made us co-conspirators in the matter of cleanliness. Hot water, and a bidet were high on the agenda.

Bill thought toilet paper was dirty, and wanted to rig up the toilet with a jet of water. Hazel, who managed the place, was willing to turn a blind eye as long as we did cheap cleaning. So we had rigged up a hot water system with a shower and a loose (very loose, it fell off on a few occasions) bidet arrangement inside a couple of days.

Success is a wonderful thing, and so to toast the new arrangement we had a celebratory drink or three. Towards the end of the cheap cask it was generally decided by both of us that life was good. And so it was that Bill, normally a shut shop, became quite talkative. I took the opportunity to ask about the Tarot Card reading business.

"Oh that" said Bill plainly. "That's a con to get women into bed, that's all. I left the Rajneesh's place in Montana because I got f..cked over by one of the body guards, ruthless sons of bitches. I kept up the jumping meditation for a time, but I just got sick of the BS. I missed the sex, however.

"When you are in that tribe, even ugly c..nts like me get lots of sex, and you don't have to do anything to get it. The women find out you're OK in bed, and that you're an Aussie: And there you go. Busy every night.

"Out here in Civvy Street I had to figure out how to get my jollies, and I struck on the Tarot Card reading biz. Gold, I tell you! Pure gold."

"But I hear the old ducks quacking down stairs about how incredibly accurate you are?" I was suggesting there was more to it with my uplifted eyebrow.

"Listen, I just use the f..ucking interpretation book, yeah? I sit them there, and go 'Oh' and 'Ah' and look as if I am studying things closely, then I pick up the BOOK, and open it up at the interpretation, and I ask the silly bitches to read it to ME! Can you believe that? They are paying me to get them to read their own fortunes from a book, one which I happened to have stolen from the library.

"I am accurate alright. I target their pussy and hit it every bloody time."

Then he stopped, and thought, "But the weird part is, a lot of that sh..t seems to come true for them. I don't know if the cards are predicting the future, or if they are manufacturing it because they believe this stuff, but it really does seem to work out as the cards fall."

Another round of drinks ensued, much laughter echoed down the plaster cracked hall, and an extraordinary tale emerged that stuck with me to this very day. It happened when I asked if any men had come for their fortune to be read.

"One" said Bill. "Only one. He saw the board downstairs and came up without booking an appointment. I answered the door wearing a towel. Hey. I wasn't expecting anyone, and the girls usually call and book. He got me as I just came out of the washroom. I told him to come back later, but he insisted that he wanted a reading NOW.

"I charged him an extra $5 for the inconvenience, sat him in the office while I got dressed. I like to have an idea of what I am looking at, so I called out before I went in to ask if there was any particular thing he wanted to know, and why was it so bloody urgent?

"He didn't even hesitate. He said he had dreams that were telling him how he was to become a famous writer, but that he also had a job promotion on the table that would take up a big chunk of his time. He needed to know TODAY what he must do.

"Well, I was thinking I had a prize F..ckwit who I could milk for lots of readings, so I go all out and put on the black robes, combed the hair, and stuffed myself to the brim with knowing looks. It was a case of Come to Poppa, sucker."

Bill stopped, and actually thought for a moment. This was unlike him, generally he was totally off the cuff and spontaneous. "Sometimes I wonder about my Soul, you know. But f..ck it. I say the agnostic's prayer and get over it."

"The Agnostic's Prayer?" I asked.

"*Please God, if there is a God, save my soul, if I have a soul*" He then smiled his winning-est smile at me, saying "Covers it all, hey?"

"Anyway, I sit down to milk the guy, and get an attack of consciousness."

"Conscious, don't you mean?"

"I know what I said. It became really obvious to me that this guy had no idea, no idea at all. Anyway, I asked the guy sincerely if he was really going to cast the shape of his life entirely on what a few colored bits of cardboard were going to tell him, and be f..cked! He said he would. He said he just didn't know, and the $25 he was paying me was the coin toss. I corrected him, saying $30 and asked for the dosh.

"I clarified it again: ' You want me to lay out these bits of cardboard, these bits of pretty paper, and you have enough faith that they will lead you to your truth?' I asked. He said he believed.

"But as I was about to lay out the cards, I stopped and wanted to qualify the question. You see, the truth is that becoming a famous writer is like picking up the Hope Diamond in the street. It's just bullsh..t so I suggested he make the question less narrow. Like, if he was going to become a GOOD writer.

"I mean, I really tried to explain that he was asking a question where to get an answer that was anything but NO was next to f..cking impossible. But a GOOD writer, that's possible. You can work at becoming a good writer. Or maybe he might become famous. That was possible as well! But you asking to become a Famous Writer? That's asking for lightning to hit twice at the same time AND be rich, good looking and popular.

"But the prick was sure of what he wanted to know, and what I, naturally enough, thought was that it was just another typical public servant who hated his job and wanted some feeble excuse to get out of it, so he could go on the dole. I figured he was just a mad prick, so I took his money, laid out the cards, and this time *I* read from the f..cking book."

"Well ... what was the interpretation?"

"F..ck the interpretation. I told him the omens were very interesting, that a person was appearing soon in his life, someone he would marry, and that he would have three beautiful children and have a happy life."

"No seriously, I want to know what the cards said." I replied.

"Well, here is the weird part of the trip. They seemed to say that he might actually just become a famous writer. I mean, I have thrown these things thousands of times, and this was the only time I ever got something that added up to this type of answer." Bill just looked off to the distance, and stopped.

"So... Did you tell him? I asked, calling him back.

Bill returned with a wicked smile and a fateful laugh. "F..ck no! He would have quit his job, ended up on the street and come back a year later to jab me for lying to him. I don't want his problems."

"But the cards said…"

"F..ck the cards," said Bill. "If he is going to become a famous writer no cheap drunk tarot card reader is going to stop him. Who f..cking well knows! I I said he was going to make it, I may have even stopped the prick. No bugger him, for $30 he gets a $30 reading."

"What was that about paying peanuts?" I interjected.

"Ex-f..cking..zactly…" Bill swung his arms in the air going "Oh Oh Oh" like a chimp. "We are all just f..cking arrogant monkeys!"

McDinky's

I had run very low on cash, and needed to find some employment. I read an advertisement for a burger company (let's call them McDinky's) that was looking for trainee managers. I call up and apply, and am booked in for a few days hence. Spin forward to the meeting.

It was all going rather well. Clearly the man doing the hiring liked me, as I was in a tidy suit and tie, clean cut, well mannered, just the sort of person who would fit in. Then came the small talk part of the interview, where your social skills were tested. So, I lead in with a simple observation.

"I have friends who have been McDinky managers in the past, and they in fact recommended that I come along and talk with you here today. (The man nods in agreement) The thing I have noticed is that, even though they have moved on to other areas, they still are very loyal to McDinky's."

Now, I was not sure how the fellow would respond, but what I got in return was extraordinary. A steely look comes over his eyes, all humour vanishes, and his mouth becomes quite grim. The pen he held in his hand as he talked now comes crashing down to the desk like a judge's gavel. Thump thump thump it goes as *he makes his next series of points.*

"Loyal!" he exclaims. (thump of pen number one) *"Loyal! My oath we a LOYAL!"* (thump number two) *"I am McDinly's!"* (pen thump number three) *"My wife is McDinky's!"* (thump again) *"My children are McDinky's!"* (thump thump thump ... meaning, I presume, three children) *"Our WHOLE FAMILY is McDinky's!"* THUMP!

SNAP! The pencil breaks in two.

The man looks up. He knows he went a little too far, but he doesn't like what he sees. I can tell he is unhappy because his face has lost the religious fervour, and now looks more like a very cross parent.

You know how it is when we are presented with absolute absurdity. I really tried not to laugh. I knew if I laughed, the job was gone. But you know how someone looks when they are really struggling not to do something that is normally involuntary? It doesn't matter how hard you bite down, it's like a sneeze, your face twists up, and everyone around you knows.

He knew, and he wasn't pleased.

I had insulted his religion with my mockery, and trying not to laugh like this meant that I KNEW it. I didn't get the job.

I guess I was really not McDinky material after all.

INITIATION

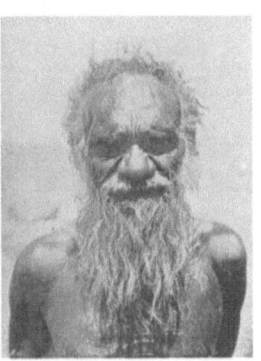

There is a place on the highest Southern ridge of Kangaroo Valley, NSW, Australia that I was shown by a local many years ago. It had always stayed in my thoughts, I was not sure why, but it was a special place. Here, for untold thousands of years, the Aborigine used to come to sharpen their flints, made arrow heads. By the look of the deep grooves in the wet rocks, they had done this in that spot since well before human memory.

I was at a loose end that summer. Don and Yvonne Locke had invited me to look after a café they had just bought at Kiama, so having nothing else to do in Sydney but share a house with a mad cat woman (honestly, I did) the option of a nice seaside residence and paid work was not hard to follow up on.

I had been there only a few weeks when I started to thinking about Kangaroo Valley. I swear it was calling me. Then, one day, for no particular reason, I had a really strong impulse to go there. I hopped on the motorbike and took the hour long journey down to find that remarkable stone shaping place again.

It was not so easy to find as I thought, and a good 2 hours had passed before I had my road bike hopping over the last of the bush ruts and onto the high stone ledge I had been shown some 10 years earlier. It had not changed at all. The atmosphere of eternity pervaded the place, and I could still feel the old people carving slowly away as they drifted in and out of the dreamtime.

Then I realised how lost I had become in my own dreaming. I had only 40 minutes to get back to work. How stupid of me to cut things so fine, now I was sure to be late. I went to put the bike gear back on, but then I sensed a presence. Who can say how this happens, but I clearly felt something, and turning around a tall, traditional aboriginal man was looking at me, looking hard at me.

I felt his eye had nailed my heart, and I flinched. He said, directly into my mind, not with words. "You are not good enough."

What can you say when a mysterious apparition appears and tells you that your batting average is below par. I thought "Weird" and went to get back on the bike to get to work, but I was curious. I turned around and asked "Why? Why aren't I good enough?"

The old man laughed, and said "Well, maybe you are." And with this he vanished. That was it! I was alone again. Scratching my head I made my way back to work, and knowing I was already late I thought "killed for a sheep as a lamb". So I stopped to have a shower, and get dressed before heading in.

The strangest thing is, I somehow arrived to work on time. I can't explain this to you, and neither can I say that anything changed in my life from that moment on, other than to say life always changes, and that maybe this had something to do with it. But it led me to writing a curious story, which I would like to share with you now:

Journey to the Mountain

Jonathon was born to be a minion. His father, and his father before him, had served as shovel men at the base of one of the great pyramids of society, and so too was his own destiny written. He was carried by his mother, as was the custom, until he was old enough to stand with his nose out of the horse manure (that covered every inch of his world) and at the earliest possible opportunity, Jonathon was given his first shovel.

At first, it was used just to clear some breathing space for himself, and to protect him against the waves of horse manure that a passing pyramid might stir up in the ever-present slop. Thus it was that Jonathon, and other minions like him, first learned to fend for themselves. And so it may have remained for his whole life, except for an extraordinary event that happened near his sixteenth birthday.

In Jonathon's world, all was organised. There were many tiers to his society, ranging from the lowest of shovellers, such as his family and himself, to those who had earned the right, through birth or through sheer effort, to rise out of the ever-present horse manure and get themselves on the shoulders of the shovellers.

How high could you rise? Well, the sky was the limit for the ambitious soul. Why, perhaps a person might rise to become one of the rare "top men"! These were the ones who sat at the very top of the pyramid, and gave instructions as to what direction the pyramid must go. These instructions were handed down, and down, and down to the shovellers, and with a pointing of a finger, they would duly shovel in the direction they were shown.

This world of itself was an impermeable grey. Horse manure for a base, and all else was grey for daytime, or black for night. Nothing else existed but the pyramids, and there were many of these. All served but one function, which seemed to mostly be a competition as to how fast they could shovel through the manure.

Naturally, the higher your pyramid, the greater importance you attained. Even a lowly shoveller would snortle when a small pyramid tried to compete against 'his' pyramid. No, you needed a goodly size structure to succeed in this place.

Jonathon was still learning the ways of his world when it happened. He was an "advance shoveller" which is how the young were trained. They had to shovel in advance of their pyramid, and lessen the depth of the horse manure so that the pyramid behind could move more swiftly.

There were three main trades that the bottom rung of the pyramid employed. These were the Shovellers, like himself, the Pickers and the lowly, desperate Carriers. The pickers had possibly the easiest job because they walked where the manure was at it's thinnest in the middle of the pyramid, and they collected the pretty stones that were passed on up to the higher ups. No one knew why the higher ups wanted stones, but the clear sparkling ones were the important ones. If the pickers did well, extra food was sent down to all.

The Carriers at the back did most of the supporting. The bulk of the higher ups stood on their shoulders, and it was they who barked their orders to the lower ranks. It was considered the worst of fates to be a Carrier, because they were the ones whipped and scolded should there be any sort of shifting that caused a concern to the Top Man.

Jonathon was not unhappy with his life. He had respect, his parents loved him, and he was on track to be accepted as a main shoveller for the pyramid. That was when his life changed for the first time. He and some of his friends were shovelling away in front of the main pyramid when, in the distance, a shaft of light broke through the ever present gloom, and revealed a definite shape in the far distance.

It was an incredible sight, one that caused Jonathon to stop shovelling and gawk in jaw-dropping amazement. There seemed a different type of pyramid in his vision, miles off into the gloom. But it was not a human pyramid; it was made of something solid. He had never heard of such a thing, apart from the story that when you died you were taken to the sacred place called "Solid Ground". Could there actually be anything that had raised itself out of the ever present horse manure?

He asked his friends to look up and see the incredible sight, but they snortled, "Good trick Jonathon, get us into trouble for daring to look up, sure!"

Then it was gone. The grey returned, and all there remained was his shovel and the horse manure it was meant for. But the incredible image stayed in his thoughts like some immovable greatness. Each night in his dreams it would come back and haunt him until one day he had to call out to his mother who was shovelling nearby. "Mother, is there anything else here you have discovered beside pretty stones in all your years?"

"What do you mean, dear," she called back. "Anything else? What else could there be? Shovellers shovel, the Pickers pick, the Carriers carry. That's it my young boy. "

"I mean mother, in all your years of picking have you ever come up against something that rose out of the mud? Something like a pyramid, but one not made of people?"

"I have never head anything so silly in all my born days, child. Where did you get such a strange notion? We know our job, and that is what we do. What good is it for you to think of anything but the perfect art of shovelling, child?"

Jonathon realised that it was something he had better not speak about any more, or his mother may just call the terrible Thought Police. He had seen it on a few occasions, where the odd shoveller had decided to stop shovelling, and just stand in the horse manure, ignoring the pyramid.

The Thought Police arrived within minutes, summoned by some unseen person, and they would harass and harangue the poor soul until he got back in line. It was a shocking social disgrace, and anyone who had such an indignity thrust upon them was treated with contempt. A shoveller was only meant to shovel, not get lost in some daydream. Such a thing disrupted the entire pyramid, and your team might lose the race if your people started doing this sort of thing.

But the image he had seen just would not go away. Jonathon practiced with his shovel every day, trying harder and harder, trying to drive the image from his thoughts. Each day he would shovel, and shovel and shovel, wanting to escape the notion through wearing it out, yet each night it would return.

In due course he grew up, and as fate would have it the frantic shovelling of his youth had made him one of the top shovellers of his pyramid. He was in the lead group, the ones who took the first orders, and he made his parents proud.

One day, as the lead shovellers were being handed down their scraps to eat from the ones above them, Jonathon noted the stirring of what looked like a storm in the distance. He had seen this dreadful occurrence as a child, and greatly feared it might be upon them again. The storm was a downfall of rain that could lift up the level of horse manure with an evil flood of water. It could even drown the young ones if they were not picked up in time.

"STORM!" he called out! Jonathon pointed in the direction where the grey seemed to be lighter, and then a remarkable thing occurred. A great jagged flash came from the sky, and a huge shape that clearly soared high out of the manure was lit up. My goodness! Jonathon thought to himself. It's the shape in my dreams! It IS real! His heart pounded and he shouted "Look! Look there!!"

Of course, by the time the others had looked up the lightning flash was long gone and all there existed was the every present grey once more. "I can't see a storm" a voice above him spoke, "Shut up and keep shovelling!"

Jonathon knew what he saw, and he knew they were shovelling right into it. But he was a good shoveller, and said no more other than to pass a message down the line to the mothers to get ready to pick up the young children, if needs be.

In all worlds, at all times, gossip is king. The whisper of a potential storm had taken hold, and despite the urgings of the top people, the pyramid started to slow. For the first time in his existence, Jonathon could see an opposing pyramid gaining on them and his own house faltering to almost a standstill.

Word had passed on up to the Top Man that someone had called a storm, so he sent down orders for this trouble maker to be brought up. Thus it was that for the first time in his life, Jonathon was called to the top. He had to somehow climb over the people above him, and following his orders, went higher and higher until he got to a shocking, dizzy height. His stomach could barely contain the fear and he drew up to the very top of the pyramid, where before him sat the highest one: The Top Man.

"What is this storm nonsense shoveller? Your job is to SHOVEL, not to look up. How DARE you call a storm you insignificant swine. Look! Look out from here. Can you see a STORM?

"No Sir," Jonathon mumbled. "I can see nothing but grey."

"EXACTLY. Nothing but grey, beautiful textures of grey. No storm, just the wonder of our exotic and marvellous world of grey. Now go down and declare to all shovellers that you were WRONG. Go down and admit your wrongness and beg their forgiveness and then worm, then you go to the back of the Pyramid."

"But, but," Jonathon stammered, not able to get the words out. This was the greatest of indignity, to be sent to the lowly, worthless place where not even your shovelling was of any use. All you did was carry the greatest of weight, because all the pyramids were stacked with the Shovellers leading the front, Pickers in the middle, and the Carriers at the back. He was no longer a shoveller any more, but the lowest of the low; A Carrier. What a fall from grace, what a shock to his mother, what a shame to his father.

His stupidity had forced him in that single, brief moment to lose a whole lifetime of effort. He was now the lowest of the low, and destined to remain there forever. No one ever left the realm of the Carriers.

Humiliated, he climbed back down, and did as he was ordered. He told everyone he was wrong, and taking his shovel, the one true friend he had carried with him his whole life, Jonathon went to the back of the pyramid to carry the heavy burden as ordered. The shame was unbearable, the fear was even worse, because he HAD seen the storm. He HAD seen the pyramid that was not of people. What's more, they were all still shovelling right into the maw of the beast.

The momentum of the pyramid began to pick up. Mother's put their children down again, cursing the fool who wasted their time and caused them to falter. The opposing teams pyramid had gained many yards on them, so everyone heaved to and worked harder and harder to pass them. "That fool" people muttered as Jonathon shuffled his way backwards, transferring the weight of the feet above him from shoulder to shoulder as he made his shameful exit from head shoveller to rear carrier.

Saying nothing, numb from the harsh criticism of the Top Man, frightened by the height he had gone to, and nervous about the upcoming storm, Jonathon's mind swam in confusion. His world had fallen, collapsed like faulty pyramid. Yet from his position at the very back he could see things in a different way.

The ones that went before had shovelled the manure so effectively that there was but inches beneath his feet. Yet behind him a great wave followed in the wake. It was the manure slowly swirling back in to the cleared hollow the pyramid had created, and it was a thing of curious beauty.

Of course, all those years of shovelling made Jonathon extremely strong, so for him the duty of carrier was as nothing. It gave him time to think, to try and gather his thoughts and to question why. Why, for instance, did they need to shovel and race against the other pyramids? Of course, there are no easy answers to the great questions of life, but now he was a mere carrier he seemed to have far more time to think and wonder.

That was when the storm hit. A storm in the manure is a terrible thing. The water that falls from the sky rushes over its surface like a demon, and all children with their noses just above the surface are swallowed by its evil fury. The screams from the mothers doing the picking reached him well before the water arrived, and then it hit. It came in a torrent, carrying with it shovellers and pickers, and taking out the feet of the carriers. All were crying and grasping for their children, and then Jonathon saw the most evil thing he had ever witnessed: The pyramid collapsed. This was the nightmare of nightmares that all his life he had strived to avoid. People were screaming, All the top people, third rankers, fifth rankers! All were strewn and tossed into the midst of the commoners. All had been cast into the muck. The whole thing had toppled.

Off to the side, the other pyramids were also falling down in dismay. Screams and horrors reached his ears and deafened his mind. All around him collapsed, and from his position at the rear it looked as if the entire world itself had fallen down.

Then is happened again! A flash of light split the sky, and in the distance the "pyramid that was not people" stood there, resolute, unchanged, unharmed. It could not be ridiculed this time, it could not be ignored. "There! There! Look over there! The eternal pyramid!" Jonathon shouted.

But no one heard him, no one even looked. All were struggling to survive, and see after their own. It was a total catastrophe. Yet it was also a release. It was also the call to action he had dreamed of, and Jonathon knew in that instant that he had to go. He had to leave now before he lost his sense of direction in the ever present grey. He finally knew with absolute certainty where it was, and now, he knew he must go there.

As he made his way through the jumble of souls that were once his pyramid, he saw his mother, weeping. Going up to her he said, "Mother, I have seen the great pyramid. I have seen it. I saw it when I was a child, I saw it when I called out about the storm, and I have seen it again just now. I am leaving, I am going to find it, and then I will come back and take you there."

His mother looked in horror. "No!" she said "The storm has confused you Jonathon. The shock of disgrace has affected your mind. You know what will happen if you go out there alone. You will grow tired, and without others to hold you up, you will fall asleep and drown in the manure. Don't do it Jonathon. Don't go!"

"I have to go, mother. I know what you believe, but I know what I have seen, and I must go!"

With this he surged off in the direction of his vision. Of course, his mother, completely dumbfounded by her foolish child, finally she did what she had to do. She did what she had dreaded would be needed ever since his first questions at age sixteen. She called the Thought Police, and pointed them in the direction he had gone. He would be ruined his whole life when they were done with him, but at least he would be alive.

Jonathon was shovelling for all he was worth when he first heard their calls. He did not know if his mother would do it, but she had. It was the dreaded Thought Police. "You have nowhere to go" the words called out, tearing into his soul. "When you leave this place, you will have no friends, you will be lonely and when you come back you will be laughed at. Don't do it Jonathon. Come back now before it is too late."

The shoveller almost stopped. A paralysing fear had crept into his bones. What if he never found this place? What if he died alone, drowned in manure?

But his vision propelled him, and he set his arms to the manure, and surged forward.

Now the Thought Police are powerful, but to try and catch a lead shoveller in full swing is all but impossible. With the pyramid collapsed they knew they would have to get back and bring order back out of the destruction, and begin the slow process of rebuilding. It had happened before, in times past. And of course, in a collapse the top people could be hurt and many shovellers and carriers killed, so they had to get back.

Instead, they sent on their most senior, cunning man, who followed the hollow trail left by Jonathon. So it was that just one thin voice pursuing him. "You know Jonathon, it is vanity to imagine you can do things on your own. It is an evil thing you are doing. Think of the shame you have brought to your family. Imagine what people will be saying about you. First the fall from Lead Shoveller to mere carrier, and from here what will be left for you?

"You must come back now and try to salvage what is left of your life. It may not be so bad because it will be recognised you DID call the Storm correctly. You may even be praised, you may get your role back. But if you keep going now, this is the end of you."

Jonathon shovelled with ever greater gusto, despite the promise offered to him. The words dug in and bit his heart. It was true, if he went back he would be praised. He would be respected once again. The ignominy would be erased and he would get his status back. His mother would be proud, his friends would cheer. Yet that would be the end of the vision.

He knew if he turned back now, when he was so close to the great pyramid, then that would be it. He would never have this chance again, and in his mind it was better to die trying to achieve the vision he had held since childhood than even be granted the status of Top Man on the pyramid.

The Policeman must have sensed his driven energy, and seeing the hollow before him lessen, he knew the mad fool had chosen to go ahead to his certain death. Casting his most lethal thought, he said directly into Jonathon's brain. "Jonathan! Jonathon, listen to me. Imagine what people will say when I come back without you? Imagine how your mother will feel? Just think for a moment. Just stop and consider the consequences: *What will your neighbours think?*"

The policeman paused and listened. If this did not stop the man, nothing would. Surely enough, the shovelling halted. The regular "gloop gloop" of the shoveller paused. Had he done enough? Had he saved this poor deluded soul?

Then the clear, certain slosh began once more. Gloop Gloop Gloop. But it was fading, not getting stronger. It was clear that Jonathon had failed to even consider his neighbours, let alone the consequences for his own mother.

Perhaps the fool deserved to die.

ALONE

It was a horrifying business. Water from the evil storm still raced across the manure, making each step uncertain. The further Jonathan got from the cries of dismay and disorder, the greater the silence and the more intense his loneliness became. Tears were falling across his cheeks, that last call had almost done it. To think of how his mother would now spend a lifetime of misery, listening to passing comments about her lunatic son, had almost turned him about.

The Thought Police were hard and spoke the truth, but they had not seen what he had seen. They had not dreamed what he had dreamed. They could never know the vision, and even if they did, they would not accept it as real. The only reality was your pyramid, and there was nothing outside of this but death.

His heart was breaking. How could he have done this to his family? How selfish was he, leaving his duty like this? And even if he succeeded, the thought remained with him, he still had no idea of his purpose in all of this. After all, even if he did find the incredible place, what then? The pointlessness of it all swept up and over him like an evil wave of water, and he stumbled into the manure.

Struggling to his feet again he realised it was true. Soon he would tire out. One man against the manure was an impossible battle. You needed the pyramid, you needed your friends to hold you up, to support you. Out here in the wild, the only certainty is your death.

He might have stopped right there and then. Jonathan might have just given up completely, and allowed himself to be swallowed by the muck, but as if one miracle that day were not enough, another appeared.

A ray of light broke through the clouds and shone like a beacon to a place directly before him. It shone clear and bright on the great Pyramid that was not made of people. Though he had been exhausted by his escape from the Thought Police, though he had been submerged and surrounded by his fears, and almost defeated by the storm, suddenly it was as if none of this had ever existed. With renewed energy, Jonathon took up his sturdy, trusted shovel and dug forward for all he was worth.

He dug and threw his way through the manure like he had never dug before. Like a man possessed, his singular vision polarised his arms, his mind and his heart to but one goal. The Great Pyramid was everything now. He realised there was no going back, no changing of the past, no repair of the present. There was just the Journey before him.

All day, all that night, and into the next day he shovelled. His arms burned, his eyes grew like lead, and his heart beat like a drum to burst. But shovelling was his life, and nothing was stopping him now. Finally he realised that the manure was no longer so deep, the shovelling not so hard. Instead of being waist deep, it was just up to his knees. In fact, he could sit down and still be able to breath.

Jonathon realised that he had come to a place where he would not drown, so he sat and discovered he could lift his knees up and get his head resting on his hands. And so it was that he finally slept. He slept all the rest of that day and into the night, when a cold breeze woke him.

Shivering now, he experience cold for the first time in his life. What was this strange place he had come to. Perhaps he had died, and come to the afterworld? For whatever reason there seemed an unearthly light shimmering in the gloom. The night was not completely black and in the distance there seemed an immense, powerful shape looming on the horizon.

Jonathon knew that shape. He had seen it in his dreams. It was the great pyramid. But another miracle there was before him! A round globe hung high in the sky, and it seemed to shine a light upon the night. Jonathon had no idea what a moon was, and had no idea that in this place the clouds were not as thick as the manure plains where he had been born and lived. All he knew was that his goal was before him, and to his amazement, he could move forward without having to shovel now.

This was an incredible experience, just being able to walk forward without shovelling your way. It was so easy, so free! With the manure only to his knees the whole of life became a floating, joyful experience. What a heaven this place was! Who could have ever imagined a life so different to being a shoveller in the pyramid?

So it was that Jonathon made his way forward, going towards the silhouette of the Great Pyramid. As the day arrived, many hours later, the level of manure had almost vanished entirely. It was barely ankle deep now, and the great vision of his youth was clearly before him. What is more, a new light, one that was dazzling and hurt his eyes started to appear. A warm, burning sensation was on his skin, made by the bright light that had appeared in the sky.

This miraculous place was beyond anything Jonathon had ever imagined, and he savoured every step until at last it happened. He was no longer walking in manure, but upon a solid ground. His tender feet felt every step, and it seemed hot to walk over, but there were now miracles beyond imaginings, and they were everywhere. These hard sticks stuck out of the ground, and they had a green cover you could sit under. You could cool yourself here, and sleep with no fear of manure at all.

His skin started to dry, and the manure that had been on him his entire life started to fall off. He felt vulnerable, exposed, yet exhilarated and free. In the distance, another person was walking, so Jonathan called the fellow over to ask him what this was. "I don't know" the man said. "I came here after the storm. I was lost and stumbled over this place. Someone I met called it 'the island' and down the way there is this door to some secret place inside. But I was turned away. I wasn't good enough."

"What do you mean, not good enough? Not good enough for what?"

"I have no idea," said the man. "There is a queue of people trying to get through this door, but no one is allowed in."

"What are you going to do?" Jonathon asked.

"I just don't know," the man said, dazed. "Maybe I can find my pyramid, and maybe they will give me back my place third from the top. Or maybe I will be sent down to be a Fifth or worse. I just don't know," and with this he wandered off.

My goodness, thought Jonathon. A Third from the Top was talking to me as an equal? And what's more HE wasn't good enough? What chance have I got? However he had been told of a doorway further along this "island" place, so off he went to see what he could find.

Surely enough, after just an hour's walk he arrived at the doorway. It was a simple affair, nothing extraordinary beyond the fact that everything was extraordinary. At a place where the ground rose up there seemed a passage through to where the great pyramid seemed to live. A hundred of more people were queued up to go through, but each in his or her turn was turned away by this extraordinary creature that could fly. It flew around in circles when someone approached, and it called out "You are not good enough. You can't come in here!"

It called this out to every single person that came up to go through the door, and every person turned away. Shoulders down they trudged back to wherever they had come from. After many hours, and after watching repeat after repeat of the same performance, finally it was Jonathon's turn.

Sure enough, despite all his hopes to the contrary, the thing the people called a Clown Bird did to him, exactly what it had done to every other soul who had approached that day. It was an amazing creature to a person whose life to this point had been determined by shades of grey. The Clown Bird was all colours you could imagine, festooned in a riot of wild, unabridged brilliance. It hurt the shovellers eyes just to look upon it. Then, fixing him in the eye, the bird said, "You're not good enough. You can't come in here!"

Jonathon could not believe it, and didn't move. The Clown Bird just repeated itself, "You're not good enough. You can't come in here!"

"But WHY?" He asked, and then on impulse he thought that it must be because he had spent so long in the manure. He stripped off all his clothes and threw them away, and said "Look I can be clean! I can wash off my past, and start anew. Look I am prepared to leave everything behind. Now am I good enough?"

But the Clown Bird was unrelenting. It just looked at the naked man and said, "You're not good enough. You can't come in here!"

What could he do? He HAD to go inside. There was nothing else left for him in this world but to go through this door. Maybe he needed to prove he was worthy by showing how well he could work? Maybe this was what it was about. So he held up his trusty shovel, his friend from his earliest times, and said. "Look, I can SHOVEL! I am a really good shoveller!"

The bird, seeing the large shovel being waved at it, flew away with a squark, leaving Jonathon alone in front of an open door. Well, he thought, I guess that means it is letting me through. So in he walked.

As soon as he passed, the Clown Bird returned, and resumed it's chant with the next person, "You're not good enough. You can't come in here!"

INSIDE AT LAST

There he was, standing naked in what he had heard people calling sunlight. The bright globe in the sky was painful to his eyes, yet through his squint he realised he had walked into the most incredible vision of his entire life. He had no names for anything as yet, but over time he was to learn it all. Here there were beautiful soft green fields, gardens, cobbled paths, quaint houses and wonderful village full of people who did not stand on each others shoulders.

Each person was free to be themselves, and had a life they could share or not. Everything here was all what you chose to do, or not. When he first walked through the door, an elderly man had seen him, and called him over, asking what had brought him to this place. Poor Jonathon was so overcome, he could barely talk, but eventually he managed to get out his story.

The old man was a tailor, and took the young man to his home and taught him the skill of cloth making. He was getting too old for carrying things, so he gave Jonathon the job of taking the clothes he made out past the Clown Bird to meet people who came up from the various pyramids to buy goods. It seemed that because of all the shovelling that people did out in the manure fields, it was really to find those pretty stones they picked up. These were very valuable, and this was the real reason the pyramids constantly travelled about.

Who would have guessed? The island was where all the shovels, clothes and food for the people came from. So much did Jonathon learn in this new place, things that that changed his world view forever. Soon his past became a bad dream, and yet every day when he met the pyramid representatives, every day he was faced with the same dilemma.

He longed to go back to his pyramid, to see his mother and father, and to tell them about this incredible place. But he knew he faced a paradox, because if he made the journey back, if he struggled back through the manure with his trusty shovel leading the way, and even if he could find them, what would happen then? What would the people of his pyramid say when they saw good old Jonathon, covered in muck?

They would simply look at him, and see the obvious. To them, he would be just another shoveller all covered in manure. They would hear his story, and they would laugh. They would say he had lost his mind. "If you had found a place not covered in manure," they would say "then why are you covered with manure? It doesn't make any sense, no sense at all." And then the Top Man would send him to the back of the pyramid for being a trouble maker, and order him to hold up the tribe.

He knew now, of course, that the Top Man didn't want the lowest rungs knowing anything about this place.

He had no answer for this other than to wait each day to see if someone he knew had bothered to look up, someone who had also caught a glimpse of a far off promise and followed their dreams.

In this marvellous place there was only one rule, which was that you must do what you agreed to do, and that at the same time you must respect another person's business and never interfere. This included the curious Clown Bird. In fact, Jonathon was clearly told that he must never interfere with the Clown Bird's business.

Here he saw another paradox. Despite the fact that every day he himself walked in and out of the doorway to the outside, always going straight past the Clown Bird's squawking, and despite the fact that people constantly saw him go straight past it, rarely did anyone follow. He never did quite understand this.

Jonathon asked the old man as they sat making clothes one day, "What can I do? I would love to bring my parents to this place, but if I go to them, they would never believe me."

The old man looked at him quietly, and said, "You are really trying to find an answer to the Paradox of Sharing. I share with you all I have, and you share with me what you have. This is how life works in a village. How do you explain this to a person who has never shared? You just cannot, they do not have the ears to understand. And there is no answer, other than sharing is good. When the heart is open, the truth is clear. When it is shut, all you can see are your own fears.

"Jonathon, just be grateful you managed to follow your dreams and come to this place, that's all I can really say. All are welcome should they find their way to us, but they themselves have to look up, and trade their fears for their dreams. That's all a person needs do, look up, see the new world, and make their way there.

"No one can do it for you. That's just the way it is."

THE GREEN GLASSES: Part Two

Death had taken a holiday. It would not have been thought possible, but Albert finally tired of the orgasm that another's death provided him. It had been so unrelenting, so constant, that the sheer joy had burned his senses.

The glasses were a permanent fixture now, to the point that he had forgotten what the "real" world looked like. Even if he took them off, the glow of the energy remained for hours, and possibly it was that the rays of light created by these incredible tools of destruction had changed his chemistry.

Certainly he didn't need sleep, or even need food. The heightened awareness hummed like a battery, powering his whole being with a clarity and focus that, for the last three months, had completely taken over his existence. Vague questions seemed to occur to him, in that there must have been other Deaths in the wings. There must be others because he barely left this city, and was kept busy 24 hours a day.

But as much as it was exhilarating, each moment reminded him of the complete state of aloneness he lived within. He used to enjoy the company of children playing in the parks, but he no longer tried to speak to them because occasionally an adult, a grey shapeless creature, would come up and ask what he wanted. Once or twice he felt compelled to answer, trying to wake their small minds, but they would get nasty. So he might lift up their energy to the point that they passed on, or not. At first it was done in the hope of raising their vision to his level, but then he became somewhat spiteful that these minions would dare questions his actions, so they died.

Unlike those who were truly ready for him, these souls gave him strange accusing glances as they were taken away into the light. Albert felt this was an unwise course to continue, it felt vaguely wrong, so despite the euphoria of deathing, he governed himself to only those ready to pass on.

This particular night, however, he felt exceedingly alone. It was something he recalled experiencing when he was a shop steward in some distant past life, and he did not like the taste of this aura. It distracted him, depressed him to the point that his work had become less enjoyable and a stain of weariness began to creep in.

Where was this place? Ah yes, the nightclub near the park. The place where he first realised he was Death. He had coming here looking for a woman, but instead found orgasm and fulfilment in removing souls from their bodies. But right then and there, the impossible happened. A woman walked past him, radiant, smiling. She had the aura of a child, the body of snake with curves, and the smile of a movie star.

My God! He was entranced, fascinated, besotted. It was love at first sight. The chords of reason were bent out of proportion in the giddy twisting of love. He followed her in as she entered the club, and entered a world long forgotten. The throb of the beat and the sinews of dancers rubbing against him reminded him of a distant humanity, a place, a zone he had once almost occupied as the mere Albert, the shadow, who sat in the shadows.

He lifted the glasses, resting them on his forehead. The swirling pulsating light of the music running through the bodies of all on the dance floor lingered, and that was when the impossible happened. The rhythm took him, took his body, and moved it in ways he had not thought possible. Dance was his religion, rhythm was his God and in the distance, the Goddess he had dreamed of all his life was waiting, watching.

He was a life of itself as the music ran up and down the nerves, reminding him of the incredible joy of being merely human once more. Slowly he made his courtship, quietly, with sheer confidence brimming form his cup, he held her eyes as he made his way across the dance floor. My God, he felt impressive.

Some deep part within himself began to open up. The heat of the bodies, the smell of sweat, triggered the primitive man. The woman was everything.

As he pulsed to the beat he came up to her ear, and whispered, "You are a radiant light, a being of love, a creature of the universe. I am death, I am finality, I am the cause of all freedom."

Never being one for pickup lines Albert had no idea if what he said was right or wrong, but it was perfectly as he saw things. Somehow it worked. The woman smiled with a radiant, beaming welcome, shaking her head in astonishment, saying nothing. It was so perfect, so sublime.

Outside he could feel the birds grow silent in their dreams, and the night sky waited. He had become a God, aware of all things, yet perfectly focused on this moment. He was a part of consciousness itself. All awareness flowed through him. He was power, he was ruthless, yet he was kind, he was gentle, still he could be cruel if he so chose. He was peace amidst chaos, even as he was the liberator of madness, the Pandorian Box itself.

"Your very breath is fire," he said to her.

"Hello stranger! Great line." she said, still smiling.

"You are the perfection of woman, the end of existence, the beginning of everything. You are the chosen, the Queen, the honey that draws the bee."

Albert felt a rough hand push him. "Piss off loser" a course voice said. Looking up, Albert, still with glasses up on his forehead, saw a huge grey shape had moved between himself and the woman. "Who the F..ck do you think you are wimp? Trying to chat up my woman right in front of me. I am gonna break your face, toad."

His glasses fell from his forehead back onto his nose, and Albert saw this angry black energy shot with crimson coming at him. "You are nothing to me." he said flatly, knowing his power to remove, feeling it swelling under his skin.

"Listen up F..ckwit. If you wanna be able to continue walking let alone talking, shift your arse out of my sight NOW!" The grey creature was angry. Flares of crimson were blazing forth from where his eyes would have been, trying to burn whatever was in front of them.

For Albert it was a fly attacking a cat. He was the butcher, and this was the meat. It was a ghost, a nothing, a wastrel and no more words or energy was to be wasted upon it. Peering into the grey mass before him, Albert saw the avarice, the greed, the need to dominate play itself out in patterns. The brutal father, the weak mother, the entire wasted breath that was this strutting peacock's life. "I am not your problem, you are." He said.

"Take off yer glasses sh..t fer brains and I'll show you a f..cking problem!" The man leaned forward and lifted up his glasses. How dare he? That was when Albert realised that he was dealing with a huge man, a bodyworker the size of a Mr Universe. He stepped back, the glasses came back down, and the Ghost resumed his proper vapid form.

"You have nothing to offer me. You have nothing to offer the world. You imagine you can own this creature of exquisite beauty, yet she knows what you are. You, yourself, are nothing but flesh without intelligence, grace or respect for life. This woman is so far beyond you, and you are too stupid to realise that she had already left. She does not belong to you, she belongs to ME!"

And with this last word, a striking vehemence came from Albert, something he had never known before. His energy focused, raised itself up in a way different to his gift of death, and it surged through him, smashing the man down. He got up, stunned, and threw a large fist, but Albert just held up his hand. It was like a mirror reflecting the rage of his assailant. The blur of power energy that came from his hand swatted the ghost to one side like a sack of feathers, allowing Albert to gaze at the beautiful woman before him.

Her eyes went wide with astonished admiration. Such a small little man, yet with such power. He was so completely different with his quaint way of speaking, and she felt strangely drawn to him. Her heart beat faster, her pupils dilated, her lips swelled, her palms started to sweat with anticipation.

Yes, she was his!

Albert took her into his arms. "You are magnificence, why play with these jesters and fools? Do you not want your death to embrace you, to caress you, to free you from the pointless existence of these mortals?"

The woman could hardly breathe. The focus of energy around her had entered into her being, and was vibrating her very atoms. Life seemed everywhere, the walls reverberated, and the music took on colour that played out through the darkness of the room like a conductor instructing the orchestra. My God, this was the most incredible man she had ever met.

Albert saw the point of acceptance. He could feel her heart join his, yet he had to pause. He had to be certain it was real so he took off the glasses to look her directly in the eyes. Yes, it was love, he saw love there like he had never seen before. She was radiant with love to the extent that he did not even need his glasses to know it, to feel it, to be part of it.

Here was his everything, his dream, his goal of existence. She was the IT, the one. Foreverness sang all about her, the truth of being rang like a bell when he was near her. Here was the woken amongst the sleep walkers, the truth, the light.

"Your lips beckon and shine like a mist that dreams about the touch of its lover. Your heart beats with the melody of ancient instincts, a primordial passion that sends shivers through my Soul. You are the one. You are my Eve, my first, my last and everything in between" He stated, clear, clean, crisp, simple.

Even without the glasses she was a radiant being. He was intoxicated, gone for all money with Cupid's arrow.

"Well," she was about to speak, but Albert saw that the gathering of her thoughts dulled her being. "No," he said putting his finger to her lips. How he adored those lips. "No, say nothing. Just feel! Feel this moment. Feel the power running through the atoms."

The woman could barely breath. She had never experienced such an incredible intensity. Who was this odd little man, the one who could swat aside the world heavyweight champion as if he were a fly on the wall? This incredible, strange person had her fixed like a rabbit in the spotlight, and she loved it. It was if he could see into her soul, ripping apart any distance she once held. Intrigued, terrified, fascinated she said "I need some air. Can we go outside?"

"Absolutely," Albert exclaimed, feeling his triumph. His heart was being struck like an anvil as they made their way across the room. Memories of his human life began to come back to him, wisps of thoughts of the miserable child that lived in the twilight of his dreams, that sad little Albert who could have never hoped to catch a fish as fine as this. The Green Glasses came back to his nose, an absolutely certainty now governed every move, every action he took. Perfection, harmony and rightness flowed through every step. Nothing could stand before him and not be humbled. He was magnificent, completely in charge. There was nothing he could not deal with, no dream he could not fulfil.

As they stepped outside, several large, grey shapes came up, protesting something about causing trouble and now being dealt with. The girl seemed frightened. No, this must not be. "Let me show you just a little of what it is like to be with me, your Death." said Albert.

He allowed the familiar to flow. The first of the bouncers coming at him stepped directly into the charged air, and Albert saw him being lifted violently from his body and cast into the shadows, crushed. Dead. The other bouncers stopped in their tracks, he could taste their fear, and it felt good.

Then on instinct, on sheer impulse, Albert did an odd thing. He wanted her to know everything, he wanted her to realise the power, the magnificence he could show her. So he put the glasses on her nose, and said "See life as I see it my beloved."

"This is incredible!" the girl exclaimed. "The whole of the night is ALIVE, everything is ALIVE and connected to everything. This is just unbelievable. Hey stranger! Where have you gone?"

"I am right here my beloved. Right here beside you. Always I will be beside you!" At last, the perfect wife, the perfect one for him. At last someone who could share his every moment, and be part of his incredible power. But it seemed she did not hear him.

"Stranger?" the girl called out "Where have you gone? I know you are about here somewhere. Stop hiding, OK? Man these glasses are something else. Everything is so amazing."

She started to walk away. Albert went to follow, but his feet were like lead and she was the breeze. "I am here beloved. Right here!" She kept walking. "I am HERE!" he screamed. But she did not hear. She walked away, calling for him, and soon left him far, far behind. He kept screaming, running frantically after the beloved and his glasses, his beautiful green glasses. The exertion and the fear were stealing the beauty from the atoms, the night was closing in, and the blackness started to descend. Quaking with horror, Albert realised he was becoming a mere human once more.

His breath frosted in the cold night air, and staggered beneath the weight of his loss, Albert looked up and realised he had run back to the park, the place where all this had begun. The curious, familiar gnome was staring at him. "Do you see the problem now, Albert? Can you truly see at last?"

The next thing he remembered was the cold, hard black of a policeman pinning him to the ground, and handcuffing him as he was bundled into the back of a patrol wagon. The black aura was sucking the last of the light out of him, and slowly he drowned in the mire of convention once more.

"Jesus" the officer behind the deck filling on forms said "They are trying to tell us that this little runt put away the world heavyweight champion with a single backhander, and killed an 18 stone bodyguard without so much as a knife. That's just bullsh_t. What sort of drugs are they serving in these places now-a-days.

"Where's the damn girl he is supposed to have kidnapped? We don't need this sort of crap. Piss the guy off, and call the coroner and find out why the bodyguard died." said the sergeant, already angrily dealing with the next one in line.

"He's got no ID," protested the other officer. "We don't know who he is, or where he comes from, and these clothes were stolen a few months ago from an upmarket shop in town."

"Look at him, you wanker. A bum found some fancy clothes in a bin, decided to get all dressed up, and got himself into a nightclub. For f..cks sake, he doesn't even have any money. He couldn't even buy himself a drink. Piss him off NOW!"

And so Albert, a total shadow of his former self, was cast out into the street, and wandered back to the park where it had all started. The arresting officer, watching him walk away, said to his associate as they closed the door. "Man, I have seen some weird ones, but he is the top of the damn fruitcake."

EPILOGUE:

After a few years Albert was let out of the asylum. He was given a ticket that said he was sane; some clean clothes; a few dollars; and set upon the street. There were never any charges pressed. No one believed that a 120 pound weakling could have done anything like what happened in the nightclub, and it was generally believed someone must have spiked the drinks.

The girl was never seen nor heard of again, but then a lot of women disappear on the streets of Chicago at night. Albert was considered a low risk, and though chronically depressed, he no longer appeared to be suicidal.

When asked by the doctors if he still had those thoughts, he simply said, "You can't kill Death."

Yes, he was looney all right, but no great risk and the bed was needed. It meant just another harmless nutter for the streets. So it was that Albert tasted freedom again. Standing there, breathing the night air that was once be so sweet, feeling the moist cool breeze blowing off the park, Albert almost laughed. Instead he cried. He cried for what was lost, and for the extraordinary life he had left behind.

His friends became the alcoholics, and they loved his amazing stories, especially the ones about Albert once being death. It all made for a fabulous night's entertainment, and finally, amidst his new brothers, these stories gave Albert back some of the light he once possessed.

Then, one evening near a night club, someone called out to him. He looked up, and grew very quiet. A woman wearing Green Glasses was waving to him. "You know her? She seems to know you." said one of his friends.

"Don't know her, but I know her business." he said very quietly. "I don't want to know her, and believe me, trust me, neither do you."

Mama was hunting Satan

Mama was hunting Satan
With a blind eye towards herself
Hidden creatures lurking
In the basement, and up upon the shelf

Hairy arm of the future
Strong arm of the law
Rules! You hate the sutures
That tie you to the floor

A guilt trip is somewhere waiting
Until you free the load
A meme, a memory, a ghost
That walks a distant road

Mama's out hunting Satan
She had a tongue to whip him good
Oh, he'll linger in the roasting fury
He would, he should, he could.

Mama, if you ever caught Satan
Tell me, what would you do?
You would be sad and disappointed
Cause the glass slipper was just a shoe

The Secret of the Gloves:

T'was a fine spring day. I was practicing my hobby, attitude watching. This is where you look at someone walking by, busy with their life, and you try to see what attitude is driving them. It's the same thing as looking at people picking their noses in traffic, yes, useless but intrinsically entertaining.

Do you want to know how to watch an attitude? Hold a childlike sense of curiosity for all that comes, suspend all judgment, dispel all belief, and just watch. That's it. Anyone can do it, and I do it regularly. People's attitude shows so clearly when you get this right.

I watched the woman drinking a coffee. She sees a couple coming down the road. Almost imperceptibly she altered herself as they got closer. I see her draw herself upright, lift her breasts higher, and somehow angle the face to show her beauty. Why? If she can catch the man's eye, she wins an invisible round against another woman.

That's attitude watching in a nutshell. Looking at people being people. This day I happened to be in the Sydney CBD, walking though one of the upmarket stores when a pair of tan pigskin gloves caught my eye. I don't know why, it just happened. I guess I just liked the attitude those Pig Skin gloves gave off.

What's more, they were in a mark down box, from $50 to $14. I only had $17 to last me the next five days, but what the hell. I liked those gloves and on impulse I bought them. It was not that the day was cold, or that I needed gloves, I just trusted to my luck that things would work out, and took them home. It's not hard to figure out why. When you are poor, a small luxury like this can make you feel like you have a Rolls Royce in your driveway.

I took to wearing them about, and on some impulse I found myself holding the right hand glove, and slapping into my gloved left hand. There was no good reason for this, and it was a little pretentious.

I felt like a Southern plantation owner from before the Civil War, walking about feeling important. It just felt good to do this, so I walked all over the place, slapping the right glove into my gloved hand. Weird what we do sometimes, hey?

Some weeks after buying these gloves, around the time they began to get incredibly familiar to me, I was walking through Double Bay. Some call it Double Pay because of the price of everything there. It is a very upmarket area of town, full of Rollers and Red BMW's and Ferrari's and Porsche.

An odd thought came to mind as I walked along. I had nice clothes on, courtesy of shopping at Op Shops in good areas (avoid the down market zones for Op Shops at all costs!). I had a decent haircut, good shoes, well clipped nails. I was well spoken. There was nothing to say I wasn't a multi multi billionaire, and no one to prove I wasn't. I slapped my gloved left hand again, and realised that I was the only one here who knew how few dollars I had to my name. The fact I was in Double Bay pretty much predisposed people to believing I was wealthy, so in a sense, I was! I realised it was the gloves that had this effect on me, they made me feel RICH.

Truth to tell, I had youth, I was reasonably good looking, I was feeling pretty healthy, I had friends, a nice place to live and enough money to get by. By the standards of 95% of the world's population, I WAS wealthy.

That was when it happened. The right hand glove literally leapt from my hand and all of life moved into an extreme slow motion close up. I saw the glove moving up, starting to turn over, and as I watched an entire lifetime of incredible wealth flashed past in a micro-second. I saw everything, my whole attitude, my whole life in that fraction of a moment.

And what a Pratt I had been in that life. Money had bought me anything I wanted at that time. Women, friends, justice: I had bought it all with the dazzling, incredible wealth I had achieved.

Then the glove slowly revolved to the other side, and a different lifetime unfolded. In this one, I was desperately poor. I starved most of my life and nothing ever fell my way. Yet inside I was deeply peaceful and at total ease with myself. I had found a spiritual purpose, and my prayers and solitude were rewarded with a deep understanding of life.

Again the glove revolved, and another life of incredible wealth spoke to me. In this one, money and logic was the mainstay of my existence. Mechanically working through the obstacles of life, I chartered my way to the top of the tree, yet died a miserable and lonely man, because I had invested nothing of my heart in anyone.

Again the glove turned. Once more into poverty I had fallen, yet once again I had found a spiritual richness that satisfied the heart. And again, and again the glove seemed to turn. It makes no literal sense, but I saw a thousand lifetimes that went from extreme wealth to extreme poverty, and all in the period it took for that glove to fall to the ground. And in every single lifetime, every single turn of the glove, it took poverty for me to appreciate my spiritual richness.

Then it hit. I stood there rocking back and forth amidst the rich tapestry of affluence and influence. A Rolls Royce convertible goes past with two blondes in the front seat. A sticker on the rear bumper reads "Born to Shop".

It was all about things. This place was full of people who believed life was all about things, and who pursued them with single-minded purpose. Everywhere about me I now saw people who were running after rainbows. Surely they had rich and luxurious lifestyles to chase them with, but they sought rainbows none the less. I saw how completely fooled we, as a race, were by the weaving we had made, the one we called "success". It was the sum total of our illusions that manufacture and drive our desires.

Don't get me wrong. I am not offering anyone a solution, nor suggesting that being poor is noble. I just realised how stupid it all was. I saw how crazy our lives can become, specifically because of our pursuit of things, and I laughed out loud. I was surrounded by people who had made money their God, and it seemed just so incredibly stupid that anyone could worship these pieces of promise, these dreams of success that each dollar represents, but which governments simply print out as needed.

Inside I knew with a certainty that whatever you call this great thing, this Spirit of Life, be it truth, or God, or spirit: somehow it comes easily to those who cherish their moment, and it thins out for those who cherish their bank accounts.

But strangely enough I still like the idea of being rich. Go figure?

The Dented Bucket

The old bucket felt useless. It was no longer shiny and new, no longer the perfect bucket in God's Garden.

Once, long ago, it had been worthy, beautiful, and strong. Now it was old, tired, and ruined. It was sad and distressed and quietly sobbed to itself as, every day, God came along to use it to water the thirsty flowers.

It cried out "I am unworthy, Dear Lord to be seen by these beautiful flowers." as the Lord poured the water it contained over the flower beds. "I am unworthy to be in your presence!" it cried as the Lord went back and filled the bucket once more. But though it felt unworthy, it carried the water as needed and gave itself to the task.

Slowly the bucket realized that, despite its ugliness, it served a purpose in God's Garden. Though battered and bruised, at least he was not cast out and left to rust. Then, one day, without warning it stopped looking at its ugliness with horror. Who can say why, but the bucket no longer remembered or regretted the beauty it had lost. Finally it stopped talking to itself about it's miseries, and then it became very surprised. Why? Because God had been talking to it the whole time. God had been speaking to him quietly, but he had never heard because all his complaints of unworthiness all these many years had drowned out his voice. He had simply never heard God saying to Its bucket:

"You alone are the most beautiful thing in this garden, for without you I could not have watered and given life to all the beauty created here. Thank you for being you."

The bucket was shocked, "But surely the Sun is more important than I? And surely the rains feed sweeter water to your creation?" It cried, almost fearful of the love it was experiencing for the first time.

God beamed down "This is true. None of us are alone in the task of creation. But you play your part as a bucket so perfectly. I could never replace you, and I love you for the help you have given without complaint. Despite all your years of service wearing you down, ruining you, making your poor body so battered, you carried on. I love you BECAUSE of this suffering, not in spite of it."

"Yet I will one day soon I will rust away and be no more!" The bucket cried.

"Then, if this is to be so, I will make you a plant holder for my most special plants, the rarest plants of my garden. You will be a home for my most beautiful ones."

The bucket sobbed deeply, and the tears of ages began to flow. The pain of a thousand journey's carrying the water to the garden, the remembrance that every bump, every scratch that was given as its gift of service: all of this came forward. And the Bucket finally saw things as the Lord did: That *because* of his scars and his pain, he was made beautiful. Because of the hard life he lived, and because the nature of his so-called ugliness was created through service, he realized he was beautiful. He could, at last, cherish himself.

And then in the sweet flow of his tears of joy, a song of the deepest contentment flowed out from him. With this song, the bucket gave to the garden a new sweetness to the water. It was love, a pure, clear love of life, and living. All the flowers lifted their heads as it touched them, and asked, "What is this beauty we are being given?"

Seeing it was the tears of joy that were singing from the dirty old bucket, finally they too discovered the sad buckets true worth. They all stopped their preening, and realized with a shock, for the first time in their brief lives, that the only lasting thing in this whole garden was the bucket they had secretly despised. Finally, they stopped looking at themselves and how beautiful they were, and began to realize the secret of gratitude. They now thanked the bucket.

Of course, the bucket is still old and battered, but now its song of joy causes even the flowers, usually so busy looking at each other and themselves, even the vain little flowers look up and remember that there is only one thing permanent in Gods Garden. This is the Love we share.

Man without Place (We Be Brothers)

He woke with the smell of strange herbs running up his nose, and the sound of an Indian woman chanting. He didn't know if his eyes were open, but he could feel that he was by a river, and heard the slapping of what must be skins in the breeze.

As his eyes focused, he saw a shaft of sunlight peering through the shadows, striking the smoke, making it seem suspended above him.

He went to sit up, but as pain shot through him, he woke to the reality that all was not well. The Indian woman came over, and peered into his eyes, saying something to another woman. The other one came over, and he saw she was a white woman.

"How strange" he thought. "A white woman in an Indian Teepee"

Then he fell back into oblivion.

It was night when he next awoke. Furs were thrown over him, he could feel them on his skin and knew he must be naked. It pleased his body to feel the soft warmth they offered. The damp of the night air was curling round his face, and he could smell the fading embers of a fire.

The man went to move his arm, to scratch his nose, and the pain almost sent him back to unconsciousness. He went to cry out, but no words came. This time, as he faded back into the nether worlds, he formed a question, "Where am I?"

Who he was, or how he came to be there seemed irrelevant. There was only the tunnel of thought that he must be somewhere, this is what held him.

As he faded back to black, he saw the man who was once his father spinning him on a rope, and laughing as he fell over afterwards trying to stand up. "Know where you are boy! Fix on a point in the distance, and anchor yourself."

For him, in the here and now, he saw and held to a lone star, peering through the gap in the teepee above him. He held to it, and the spinning wheel of confusion began to settle down. And once again, he faded to black.

Music woke him the third time. An Old Man was drumming on a hand held skin drum, and singing with a low, monotonous rhythm. He remembered that sound. He had heard it so often in his youth. He remembered: his father was a trapper, and they would go for weeks at a time into the mountains.

His father knew the Indians well, and would often take his son to their events. He looked out, and saw the old man's eyes looking at him. He knew those eyes. He had seen them all through his childhood. He saw them looking through him, into his soul. And it hurt. The pain in his body was nothing to the pain he felt from those burning stakes that drove into his fear and confusion. And once more his consciousness left this place.

One Week Passes

Slowly the man came to some semblance of recognition of the world around him. The strange white woman was still there, he had no idea why, but she looked at him harshly. The Indians were far more compassionate, and treated him as one of their own.

And it seemed he was one of them. That was all he knew. Fragmented pictures of time spent in Indian camps as a child were like a jigsaw he could not grasp. He saw the picture, but the pieces made no sense.

As he came back to this world, it was clear something terrible had occurred. His body had multiple wounds, that seemed to be from a knife, but he had no connection between these and the present moment. There were only the pieces of memory: the odd image of his father, and the visits to Indian camps.

It was like drinking a soup that doesn't sustain you. You taste it, but there's nothing else.

He knew their language, though. He remembered sitting as a child, going over the names of things with a young boy, one his own age. This came through clearly. Sitting by a lake, communicating, finding the way to connect between his culture and theirs.

He remembered this as vividly as if it were yesterday, and he knew the boys name. Tahoma. He called it out in the language he learned from him, "Tahoma! Tahoma... is that you?"

The old medicine woman came over, tears in her eyes. In the same language, and with sorrow, she said words to the effect that many things had changed since that time. The man knew she was telling him that Tahoma was dead. He remembered how the Indian rarely said things directly, and that you had to grasp the feeling of what was said, more than the words.

Then she spoke directly to him, "But at least you start to remember."

Why this triggered such a sense of sorrow, he did not know.

Two Weeks Pass

He was able to sit up now, despite the fog of pain, and was able to lift a broth to his lips. He knew where he was, he remembered these people from long ago, and the journey's he took with his father. He remembered how his mother had died, and he lived in the wild with his father, hunting furs.

He remembered some of the words of his father, things that came in short bursts. "We are here as guests, son. And like any place you visit, respect the house you live in and the people that feed you." He saw his fathers eyes over the camp fire. "But this is no place for learning. You been sent a gift, boy, a lonely gift, but your dead mother's family have agreed for you to get learning down in Austin. An education means you won't have to live your whole life in these hills like your father."

He remembered saying, inwardly, that he WANTED to live his life like his father. But he said nothing. It was like a night of sorrow had fallen. Then the memories stopped. All memories ended. There was only this huge gaping crevice between that moment and this one.

The angry white woman appeared soon after, and speaking in English asked if he remembered anything yet. He didn't want to talk to her, and said in the language of the natives "I don't need your world."

Someone must have been listening, because as the woman's rage started to burn, some squaw came in and took her out of the teepee. He was relieved to see her go, and wondered why they kept her here. Yet at the same moment, he started to wonder about the gap.

An Old Man entered, the one that had looked into him so long ago, and again those eyes fixed onto his soul. This time they were gentle. "Do you remember your name?" he asked.

"I remember Tahoma. I remember my father. I remember walking the hills as a boy. I have pictures in my mind, but that is all."

"You have been damaged in body and mind." the medicine man said simply. "But nothing can harm Soul. It gives you a little each day, so gather these gifts of the past, and slowly you will be able to piece your life back together. Allow what will come to come, and know that because of your father, you have earned the right to stay here.

"It is not a gift we offer you, white man, but the repayment of a debt. Your father gave his life seeking to help us. He is honoured amongst our people, and even though we have lost out lands, cast to this place of little truth, and separated from our ancestors, we still hold to their values."

It struck him then, the old man called him a white man. That's right! Up to that point he had thought the white woman strange, now he realised he was the same. "Why is that white woman here?"

The old man grunted. "hmm... well, she is a burden we carry on your behalf. You may come to understand why, but you can cut her free at any time."

"She has such anger, it hurts me to have her visit." he said simply.

"All wounds hurt till they heal," the old man said. "If we look at the wound it reminds us of the hurt, but to remove the wound by cutting it free would only cause greater suffering."

"Then she must stay?" the man asked.

"To honour your father we keep her. To heal your mind you will need to understand her. She is the cause of your suffering, and yet may be the doorway through which you become free of all confusion. It in unknown what paths will unfold, but what I do know is that she is part of your journey.

"For now, heal. Soon you will be able to walk, and then you will decide what you must do."

He faded back to dreams. He started to remember this old man. He remembered his father speaking with him in low, serious tones, but he could not place any meaning on it, or recall details. It was all before the gap appeared, and it started to occur to him that his father sent him away for a reason.

A Month Afterwards.

He was able to walk again. The Indians had given him a name, Dreamer. He thought it must have been their humour because he was totally useless and spent most of his days now lying on a bed under trees, watching the movement of life.

The sunlight falling through leaves, playing out on the lake where the people of the village drew their water. It was an endless tinkling melody of events. And slowly it dawned on him that the women were constantly drawing water, and using it to water crops a good mile away. What a suffering it must have been for them. Then he saw how he might help. He was not allowed to talk to the wives directly, of course, but he went to the medicine woman, and said he saw a way to help the women water their crops. She looked long and hard at him, and asked "How do you know this?"

He didn't know how, he just saw a way to make their life easier, and it was a way to repay a little of the kindness given him. They may be honouring his father, but he could not sit by and be a burden. Despite his uselessness in body, and lack of memory, his mind had become sharp and aware.

In his former life he knew there were things called pipes, but it was clear these were not here. But the principle was the same. How did you make a pipe"? How could you contain water and direct it to a specific point?

Well, they had buckets and they had rope. He organised to tie a rope between a strong tree beside the lake, and a tree on the far side of the fields of corn. It needed a number of poles along the way to hold the rope clear of the ground, and this was done with teepee poles set into a "vee", with the rope being tied to these at regular intervals.

Now to make the water buckets move easily he fashioned a small grooved wheel from timber, and put a greasy axle through it. This carried a hook, that held the bucket. Now the women could lift the bucket to the rope, and pull it along rather than carry it. Each stay meant they had to unhook, and lift it back for the next stage, but it meant the crops could be watered far more easily.

The women were happy. Now three of them could do the work of 12, and they ended each day without aching tiredness. They honoured him in song, naming him as the true son of his father.

Slowly the man known as Dreamer came to grasp what had happened. These people had lost their lands to the whiteman, and been placed into a reservation. Where once their crops had been watered with regular rains, this place was much drier, and just surviving meant far more work for all.

The men had little by way of ranges left for hunting, and their rifles had been taken away. Bows and arrows are of little use unless there is something to hunt, and they had been reduced to raising pigs for meat. Even their horses had been taken, and the missionary and his wagon had become their source of flour and other essentials. But this was handed out only if they attended his services.

To a proud people, it was an insult. However, old women with dead husbands and sons had little choice. They went to the white man's church because it meant they could survive.

Dreamer wanted to go to this white man priest, and tell him how cruel it was, but the Old Man forbade it. He must not be seen by the white men, they must not know he was alive, especially the white woman who still stalked him at odd times, demanding he remember his past.

The corn grew well, that was his best answer to her.

The Village Becomes his World

He remembered that the Old Man had said how he needed that mad, white woman. But in everything he did, he sailed right past her, and did not seek any connection.

He ignored her, and he ignored her angst by looking to help his friends. They had serious concerns to deal with here on the reservation. For one, the men could not travel away into the own world, pursuing the hunt. This made them restless and uneasy. Many times he saw short tempers that were tied not to the villagers, but to their confinement. There were no horses to ride, no rifles to shoot, no place to travel to honour the ancestors and few places to hunt. But it occurred to Dreamer that they were sitting on a unique range, the lake.

He remembered how his father had fashioned hooks out of bone, and taught him to fish, and so he taught the men of the village how to hunt for meat of a sort they were totally unused to. But it gave them reason to wake up, and stories to tell of a shared experience with the other men. It was not ideal, but it eased the lives of men who had only ever hunted. Added to the bounty of the odd meat bird that they could arrow, it meant that the men, too, started to sing praises in honour of the father's son, and count themselves blessed he had returned.

In the meantime, the white woman became less angry. Slowly she became less of a burden and started teaching the children the words of English that would help them deal with the white men.

Dreamer was not to know it, of course, but his presence and the fact he must remain hidden gave the Old Man reason to forbid the young men from speaking to the ones who came seeking to trade alcohol for their Indian things. It was less of a concern, now that trapping the furs was a thing of the past, but it gave the old man a reason to keep them out.

And so a year or more had passed, and some sort of harmony had now come to the people.

Dreamer continued to help in whatever way he could. Slowly he taught the folk how to make new forms of housing. First he taught them to bend wood by steaming it, and showed them how to make dome tents that were more suitable to permanent occupation. With his limited resource he showed them how to split timbers and bend them into shapes with steam, then lock their shape into place with hide ties so that as they cooled, they made strong shelters against the elements.

And with every small detail that came to him from his dreaming, he saw another piece of his past life fall into place. He started to remember the white man's school, and how he came to know things. He remembered working out on the great plains, laying the tracks of the great iron horse known as the railroad.

He was an important man, directing the white people, finding ways over rivers and through mountains. Months at a time he lived out in the wilds and he remembers coming back to the white woman with him in this camp. They were connected, and he presumed she must be his sister, or something like that.

But that was all. Anything else that came through beyond this brought up a wall of anger, an unreasoning fierce hatred of something he did not want to see. But it played on him. What was his name then? How did he end up here? Why did they need to remain hidden? How did he receive such terrible injuries?

His fingers would run over the many scars, asking such questions. Of course, other questions were raised by those far removed from the man.

A new song started to sing itself in the white man's world. The Indians themselves had become a curiosity, because the odd government agent who arrived, expecting to find a dishevelled, dispirited community of hatred, discovered instead the opposite. People laughing, children smiling.

For some reason these people had adapted and were thriving, and the extraordinary new buildings were proof of some force at work. The children were even able to speak English. It was a wonder.

Whereas the visit from the Indian Agent used to be once or twice a year, now they would come every second month, and with the agent came white men in important hats who arrived in fine coaches. Soon the secret would be out. Dreamer and the white woman would have to leave, because, as the Old Man explained, if they were found there the whole village would suffer.

And so it was that Dreamer and the white woman were sent to the hills alone, and here, in the forced loneliness away from his people, the nut finally cracked.

It started with her. "You remember NOTHING!" she shouted to him after the third night in the mountains. "You don't even wonder how to God we both got to be in this hell? We had it all, everything, and... and ..."

He looked up. This was the first time her anger started to crack. He saw it run across her face, the surrender, the giving up of the pride. And inside that moment, he saw something long forgotten, and it surprised him ... It was a love for this creature.

She must have caught his look. It was like a woman set out on a sea of hopelessness had been thrown a line, a connection to a broken world. "You DO see ... You DO see. But what do you see?" she whispered, teetering on some abyss.

The Indian in him grunted. Yet the white man in him saw that if they were to survive out here, away from the village, then he needed to overcome whatever their history might have been. He didn't like this woman, yet he knew that at some point in his past he loved her greatly.

"I see that somehow in my past I loved you. I don't know how, because you are a creature to me, but at one point you were very important to me."

The woman was stunned. Her already white face paled even more, and she could barely hold herself up. "You ... you LOVED me?" she stammered.

He was busy twisting semi-dried gut to make strings for his bow, but inside he journeyed to a place that was once dark to him, and the door opened. "Yes," and with eyes looking to a distant shore, "I see I was never there, I was working on the rail-road, wasn't I? A specialist engineer away for over a year at a time ... I remember now.

"Oh yes... I remember now. The anger I felt when I returned to find a child that was not mine and another man in my house." Dreamer paused. There was only one thing a man would do in such a situation. "Did I kill him?"

The woman nodded, bleakly. "Yes, you killed him."

"And what of the child? Where is the child?"

She was beyond tears. These past two years had reduced her to a harsh reality, the simple truth that everything was now gone. "You killed my son. You knocked him from my arms so violently, he died. Do you remember what happened next?"

Dreamer was not shocked, he knew he was capable of killing, and he remembered now. As if standing behind himself, he saw himself as a strange man wearing an expensive white man's suit. He said something in anger. The man had started to draw his pistol, and he just reacted. He saw himself draw a sabre and strike. Then nothing. He remembers the blood gushing out from the neck. Then nothing.

"No... it ends with me striking the man with my sabre"

"You went to kill me after that. You knocked my son to the ground, and he screamed. He screamed in such pain that you stopped, and picked him up... and he died in your arms..." She broke down, collapsing to ground, heaving with tears, "my little boy... You killed my little boy..."

He did nothing, just stood there. But he remembered the shock. He remembered the feeling of utter loathsomeness running through him. He remembered now the gaping hole into which he fell.

"You just stood there … You just stood there staring, then you dropped your sword and the dead child. I was the one who tried to kill you. I was the one who picked up that sword and stabbed you so many times, and you just stood there, ignoring me like you always did.

"And then I realised what I had done. I realised you would die, and I would hang. There was nothing to do for the dead, but maybe if I got you to the Indians you loved so much, but who you ignored the same way you ignored me, maybe they could help you.

"I could not take you to a local doctor, so I wrapped you onto a sling, and dragged you behind your horse through the hills, half presuming you would be dead before I got there. I got lost in the woods, but somehow the old man found me, and took us to the reservation.

"Two YEARS I have lived with those savages, and watched you become one. And yet, though I hated you, there I saw the man I once loved. The man who gave his life to helping others. I finally stopped seeing the murderer of my child. That was when I started teaching their children. It brought me a little closer to what I had lost."

Dreamer looked at the woman, and for the first time felt compassion.

He thought of the old man, with the eyes that burn through you. He had seen the pain in them both, and kept them safe till they were ready to bear the memory of it all. These were his true people, not the white men.

They were always his people. The anger that killed the woman's lover, that killed her son, and the anger she almost killed him with, this was all one and the same frustration. It all came from being where you don't belong, and living a life of compromise between your true nature and what is expected. It was the pain of doing what you should.

"Woman," he said simply, "the past is done. Trees do not mourn the leaves they have cast off. I can see how greatly I have hurt you. You believed yourself unloved, and you sought and found love. I see this now without the colour of anger over my Soul.

"I accept your hatred and understand it now, and release you with kindness. You can find your way back to your world without fear of me following. This (he waves at the forest around them) is my world now."

She laughed with a shallow whisper. "They would forgive you." she said, "He was drawing a gun, it was self-defence and the child was an accident. They will never forgive me. A woman who tried to kill her husband, even if acquitted, has no life worth living in that world."

He saw her hopelessness. She was trapped by the circumstances of their collected rage. "What can I do for you, then?"

She sat there in the grass, beside some wild flowers, and the silence of the forest echoed with the thousand murmurs only nature can bring to your ears. A lifetime of pain started to ease, and then, with finality, she whispered. "You can give me a child."

He nodded, and bent down to hold her, but she knocked him away fiercely. "I am not asking you to LOVE me. I am asking you to give back a little of what you took."

Dreamer almost smiled. There was more Indian in her that he would have guessed.

Many years passed, they created a variety of interesting homes, using his wood steaming to bend shapes, and hides to cover them. In such a manner the former enemies raised two very happy children. Going back to trapping, Dreamer brought in the small necessities such as axes, and tools, and in due course the white man's world came in to visit them via other trappers, and the various prospectors that came into the wilds.

He traded for gold pans, and himself collected the gold in the white man's way from the rivers. He then secretly showed some young men from the reservation how to do the same. This meant that his people could now get horses and tools for the villager, which gave the men the freedom to hunt once more, and allowed for pipes to irrigate fields.

In time, Dreamer became the connection between his tribe and the outer world, and finally the link was made with the missing engineer, his wife, the dead baby, the lover, and the strange white people that lived like Indians. But that was years ago, and there was little left to be said.

A local magistrate, when presented with the matter, essentially ruled that even if murder was charged, which seemed unlikely, then the statutes of limitations, the factor of time itself made a hearing unlikely. The reality was that most white people considered that living out in the wilds like natives was punishment enough for any possible wrongdoing, and the scene of death was obviously a man with his hand on a gun being killed by a sword. The baby seemed accidental. No one knew of what the wife did to the husband.

The magistrate simply said in summation: *Res Ipso Loquitur*. It was a thing that spoke for itself.

And so they were allowed to live out their curious life, a life between two worlds.

But for those with the eyes to see, the message of this strange pairs twilight existence was clear. It was as obvious as the sign on the doorway into their cabin in the woods. There, Dreamer had carved a saying that spoke the simple truth of his life.

"We Be Brothers, or We Be Others"

Mad Rotten Fruit

Mad Rotten Fruit. Strange Fruit
Hanging from the tree of knowledge
Crow pecking with innocent eyes
like a woodpecker looking for grubs

Weird fruit. Lost in a web of weaving
that entwines upon itself until daylight is a memory called night

Sagging fruit, heavy with itself
waiting to fall, expecting doom

Mad Rotten Fruit. Falling before the fall
It whispers to itself that the way up is down
That wrong is right. That dark is light.
Sadness calling for separation from separation
Mad, and rotten with the cloying sweetness of pretence

Yet while Rome burns there is a little light?
Yes, but it is the shadow that rule
Yes, and the fall from your civilized self is hard

Mad Rotten Fruit. Fermenting stories inside until
completely rotten with its own imagining, it falls

Humpty Dumpty, and all the King's horses, and all the King's men,
and even the wall are surprised they couldn't put it together

Again

Out from the garden you are cast, away from the vine
Hope that the seed within will provide you your worth

Mad. Rotten. Fruit.

The GATHERER of the FLAX

E ach day, in the fields and beside the highway, the man could be seen collecting the flax. It grew wild by the roadside, and in the ditches and valleys nearby. A man could survive where chance, in the form of travelling carts spilling seed, had cast her harvest. For the vagabond it sufficed as an existence, for you could cut and bundle the coarse strands that grew on the untenured lands, and spread them out to dry in the sun. Each night he would take the dried flax from each days gathering, then beat it, and either weave it into rope or sell the raw material to the local weaver.

Some might have praised this soul for his industry, but this was a harsh land. Collecting flax was the habit of children and his activity was seen as akin to scavenging. He was a creature on the edge of society and the man was considered low. A slave faired better, for the most part.

Yet there was something about this man that stirred you. The rough hands, the sun hardened face, these all men shared but not that strange stare , that foreign, alien gaze. It made you feel uncomfortable. Sensible people kept their distance, for he was an outsider, a nobody with no opening to the world of society. In our modern world, he would be the lunatic on the bus, the alcoholic in the gutter, or the eccentric.

Obviously, no decent person wasted breath on this type of wastrel. "Turn the other cheek" the Mothers would say to each other if his presence were brought up at either the well or market. In Ancient Judea this meant to ostracize, and have no dealings with the person. But still, the presence of this strange man clung to the air is a haunting way. Some of the women swore he stared at them, even in their dreams. It was clear he was to be avoided. He was not even a proper Jew, but apparently one of the Essenne sect.

He was outcast, untouchable and to be ignored. But did this appear to concern the man? Not at all, it seemed. He went right on as he had for months with his lowly business of gathering the wild flax and then winding it and selling it as rope. Each sunrise found him gathering, and each evening he was in the abandoned hut on the edge of the village, weaving his rope.

Of course, the men would have spoken to him as would all men that shared a beer, but he did not frequent the betting pools or taverns, or their gambling dens. So this man had little recourse with anyone. Indeed, few but the gossips gave him even a passing thought as he scavenged in the wilderness.

Yet of course it was very different with the children. Gathering the flax, as they would be doing as well to earn a coin, the children saw him often. They loved to speak with him, and he often was seen laughing with them. They came to know and like him, for whatever the man was to the adults, to the children he was the most wonderful storyteller who always had a tale of amazing places and far off lands for any and all who had an ear to listen.

"Tell us of the time you met the bandits at that merchant town!" One would call.

"Oh, that story is days old, children." He would say, laughing at their bright open eyes. "There are so many more to tell. What about a story about the COBRA! The amazing snake that flattens it head when it is about to strike!" His hand would mimic a cobra about to strike. The mouths would open, the eyes light up, and the ears would be straining to hear every single word. And so each day the tales were told, and every story became another adventure for the children in some far off land. And there is nothing children love more that extraordinary tales and incredible creatures.

Naturally, the children did not tell their mothers about this. Little ones are wise in their own way, and they know how mothers are too quick to say "You cannot do this! The man is a stranger, and may be dangerous. You must stay away." But of course, as time went by the ripples spread out through the humdrum of village existence, and one mother after another saw how many children seemed to follow the stranger about. Strangers are not safe. One word of fear invariably breeds many and soon enough the women were up in arms at the dangerous evil that had crept into their midst.

It came to the fore on the day the Roman Aedile came to town, on his regular route supervising the granaries and checking the weights.

"He must be stopped!" they called out to the village elder. A gaggle of angry women is like a horde of wasps descending, so the elder wisely avoided the issue and merely agreed with the women, but saying, "It seems like a legal matter to me!" Thus he sent them off with their plaint to the visiting Roman.

They descended on him without warning. The Roman, already bored with his life in this provincial outpost, had no mind to deal with anything but the granaries, and to get to the next town. He did not want his mid-morning repast disturbed by a vexatious clutch of women baying for blood at his door. Even so, he went to see what the trouble was.

"He is polluting our children's minds!" they caterwauled. "He tells them of incredible strange journeys, and their hearts are stolen and they go idle all day." The women muttered their approval to each other, as they all agreed upon the evil in their midst. Naturally the Roman simply wondered how he could best get rid of this troublesome tribe of gossip struck women.

He could pass them on to no one else, so either he was forced to listen, and suffer the muttering and curses, or it was likely he would see bad reports written about him to the governor. Besides, he dreamed of becoming a magistrate, and who knows what else? It was good practice for his future dreams, so he took charge of proceedings by asking careful, deliberate questions about the matter.

It soon became clear that the man broke no law, nor had he interfered in any way with the normal processes of village life. So the Roman declared that the problem was not his. This should put an end to the matter.

"He breaks no rule, women. By your own admission, all he does is tell your children stories. Why, a storyteller we all are at some time! Further: He makes no trespass gathering flax on untenured lands. It is his right as a citizen to do so. Therefore I have no ruling except that you, yourselves, must take your own children in hand, and allow this man as much right as you would give yourselves."

Done. No nasty reports to the governor. He had the matter neatly dealt with.

The village women turned away, greatly displeased. But the storm kept brewing. After many hours of nagging, their husbands were forced to act. This time, wives pushing them, they themselves go up to the Roman to further their wives plaint. This time the hapless husbands speak. "We have ordered our children not to talk to him," they cried out as instructed by their wives, "but still they do so. We say to not speak or listen to this man, and yet he speaks to them still! He draws them in. They are bewitched by this devil!"

The Roman lifted his voice over their wailing. "SILENCE!" he roared. "Roman Law is very clear, and though you people barely deserve it, answer me these simple questions. Tell me: Does this man go out of his way to talk with these children? Does he seek them out?" he questioned the crowd.

Consternation broke out amongst those present. The rabble muttered, comparing notes that might incriminate the accused. Finally one spoke out, a wizened old crone. "He does not seek out the children, but by some dark force he draws them to him against the wishes of the parents. We claim this as grounds for witchcraft, for our children were well behaved before this man came here." This brought a rousing murmur of approval, and before him the Roman saw a thatch of nodding heads.

"But as you yourselves have stated: The children sought him out long before you forbad them to see him! I can hardly see this as a claim of some dark wizardry. Rather, it is one of disobedient children." The Roman spoke carefully and reasonably, knowing how easily he might anger the rabble before him. Villagers are like dogs howling at the moon. There is no reason for the action, but how do you explain this to a dog? If you want some peace you have to silence them, and that means feeding them. He acted to sooth over their consternation before it rose up like a snake to strike outside of the law.

He had seen it a hundred times. Crowds that begin to turn towards that ugly shade of prejudice, that then turns into the mob which authority most fears. And a mob they were becoming. Men and women were shouting accusations about the man, threatening that unless justice be done by the court, it would be done otherwise. The Roman saw they would have to be appeased, and so he arranged a hearing for the following day, sending word to the man and demanding his appearance.

He sighed. He wanted to be out of this godforsaken place, do his rounds, and get back to the relative civility of Jerusalem with his reports. But a riot the day after he left town would look bad to the governor, so he stayed.

Excitement! A real Roman court to be held in their little village! The taverns were rumbling with the whispers all night, and the women went visiting each other like a gaggle of geese, setting forth their case to all, confirming their own stories to each other, tales that clearly proved enough guilt to incriminate the interloper, the one who had disturbed their otherwise peaceful existence.

The sun shone brightly the next morning, and with the cattle lowing in the muddy green pasture surrounding the town, the Roman called the day to order. Wearing his gown of office, he sat on a makeshift Chair of Judgment, and signalled for the days event to begin. He had the chair placed into the open arena in the village square, to show how open handed he was going to be. In this way, he appeased the women with an air of importance, yet kept the matter to a local dispute.

The two bored soldiers that escorted him around the province were placed behind him, to make the matter look serious, and to protect him in case this lot turned into an angry swarm. They were dull-eyed men, near retirement, who enjoyed sneering at the crowd and fingering their swords as a continual reminder that order must be kept.

And then the man himself walks into the midst. The crowd stirred, and a few names were called, but the Roman held up his hand for silence.

A large crowd of curiosity seekers had gathered to see the man. Indeed, the fellow now held an air of mystery as he stepped out from the shadows of his personal inconsequence and into the appointed place for trial. Though most often ignored, he was well known to all by the passing acquaintance of eye contact. It had all become quite the spectacle.

Somehow, the vagabond had managed to gather clean clothes and appeared to the court well-washed with beard trimmed. He went to his appointed place, a small seat near to the dais.

Despite clean clothes, the obvious effects of the years of outdoor living showed in the nails and hands. The rough, tanned face spoke of many seasons under the sun. Lines were cast into his features like ruts on a well worn road. He sat there impassively, hardened hands linked calmly in his lap. Despite the gawking and muttering all around him his composure was completely unruffled.

The Roman was impressed. He was like every other working man except for the details. These details are in the way he sat, and the graceful manner in which he moved. There was nothing awkward about his presence, and certainly there seemed no sense of being intimidated by the crowd. Most of all, he had exceptionally clear blue eyes. Those eyes were un-dulled by circumstance, and remained bright and alert, clearly untouched by the monotony of daily life and the tedium of humdrum affairs

It was just this type of thing that the Roman looked for when judging a man's worth. This one had an air of difference. Certainly it seemed that way. As an educated man sent out to the dirt and grime of local politics, this Roman was similar to most of his brothers forced to do their duty in the boondocks. They universally despised the grubby and petty minds of all who surrounded them. Every true Roman wanted only one thing, to be in Rome.

So it was that the accused man stood out. Against the backdrop of so many village minds wrapped up in a cattle-like world of subsistence, here was a strength, a sense of presence that his would-be judge recognized. The Roman saw something that, in other circumstances, he might have wished to have known more of. But it was not to be at this moment, nor in this place.

"You." the Roman called, indicating for the man to step forward. "You have been accused of misleading the children of this village, causing them to dream and thus neglect their duties. These people say you are employing witchcraft to do so. How do you answer this claim?"

The man stood up, and unclasping his hands he spread his arms with a shrug and said, "How can I detain the children," he answered. "They are like the birds that come and go from the tree. I do not hold them, nor cause them to dream. I simply answer questions they would ask. I tell them stories of where I have been and what I have seen."

The surrounding crowd ruffled like a peacock ready to display it wares. The Roman, aware of the mindlessness of uncontrolled men, took the proceedings in hand with the full weight of his judicial manner. "That is not sufficient. What questions do they ask? And what answers do you give?" he demanded.

The man shrugged once more. "The children will ask things like why the birds sing, why the rivers run, why is the sky blue?"

"And what do you reply?"

"I say simple things. That the birds sing because they love life, and wish to add a little beauty to this world. I say the rivers run because they know that idleness in the sun causes them to become useless like a stagnant pond. I say the sky is blue because it is different from the green of tree and grass. That the Lord God made it that way so when people be of a different colour, or type, or richer, or poorer, that they could be proud of their difference, as this is how God made them."

"See!" a woman from the crowd called out. "He fills their heads with empty nonsense, dreams and imaginings. The children listen to this more than they listen to their parents, and we can't get them to obey us at all." The crowd murmured its agreement.

The Roman signalled them to order, asking further of the man. "You speak of different races. Have you travelled? Have you worked as a merchant?"

"Travelled? Yes most surely. I have travelled past Egypt, Your Honour. I have travelled to the far ends of this planet and seen much, but I did not do this as a merchant. I travelled with them, but my purpose was for spiritual study."

The magistrate felt a wrenching in the very bones of his heart. My God! Beyond Egypt! How he longed to travel to Egypt, to see the wonders he had read of there, to visit the places Plato and the old ones had spoken of. But of course, none of this showed in his face. "You appear to have no trade. How do you survive?"

"I have a trade, Your Honour. I am a carpenter, and in the past I served the merchants with repairs, which gave me free passage, and I paid for my tuition at various schools with my work. But my tools were stolen coming back to these lands, so now I earn a little money gathering the flax. I knit the flax into rope and trade this for food and shelter."

The weight of how a man can be so wronged with the judgments made according to appearance settled like a depression on the Roman. A carpenter! A mere CARPENTER had taken his tools of trade, and done so simply what any man could have done. He had journeyed freely to the far horizons.

Yet he, a learned man of significant means, was trapped as a Aedile, and compelled by duty to remain at his post. His sense of imprisonment in this miserable dustbowl of a village increased with every word this man before him spoke.

Of course, none of this showed in his face. Yet did he detect a twinkle of amusement in this man's eye? Did this lowly fellow who stood before him realize what was running through his mind? He looked more closely, and realized with shock that this rough carpenter understood. Somehow, this uneducated man had stared right into his heart, and for all the world the Roman fought to hold back a deep tear welling up in his eye.

He mentally forced himself to snap back to the matter before him. "It is clear," stated the Roman, "that you are not a burden on the public good, for you do support yourself. It is also clear to me that you mean no evil intention to the children of this village."

The Roman paused to let the words sink in, but before the crowd could erupt in anger he continued, "But I ask you, what right have you got to take children away from their duties and the way of life their parents intend for them?"

This cleverness brought a rousing murmur of agreement from the villagers. All admired the way this Roman had so tactfully dealt with the problem.

"What right has the bird to sing?" the man replied. "I simply say what I will, the children decide to listen. How does this draw them from their parents?"

The Roman once more looked deep into the man's eyes, understanding for a moment a little of the pain hidden there-in. This pain, this separation, it was his pain as well. It was everything he had suffered in life, yet more. This man's pain shone like a golden coin in the depths of a lonely ocean. The Roman was taken with a wish that he could somehow reach in and take it, hold it, treasure it for himself.

Egypt! What a journey, and even beyond, the fellow had said. What he could learn from this stranger if they had but the time. Yet he also wanted to despise him, to prove to him that the cost of his freedom was too high. He wanted to take that secret coin from this sad-faced fellow, so that he might hand it back, saying "Look! Here is the cost of your truth!" But he could not. Instead he drew the man aside from the villagers, and spoke quietly.

"I see in you, friend, a deeper wisdom. But this wisdom hurts the small minds of this place. They cannot contain it. You, by your simple words, have brought joy to the hearts of the children of this town, but when they seek to share this with their parents, the brightness of their smiles hurts their mother's eyes."

Then it struck the Roman. Could it be that this man was quite possibly educated like himself? "Can you read, and have you read Plato?" The vagabond nodded his agreement.

The Roman was shocked. This man was far more than a carpenter. He could have a position in any court. He could READ, he had travelled beyond Egypt! Why was he here? Why here in this miserable, god forsaken place?

However, the crowd was beginning to rumble. "Then remember the cave! The eyes of parents who have lived in the darkness and ignorance of tradition cannot accept the change their children bring them. Their children seek to bring home some joy, but the parents fear that this very joy will break the bonds that are both their curse and yet their security. They fear for themselves, and their children, and they fear what will happen because of change. Further: They hate you for causing this trouble in their lives. And when I leave, they will kill you."

Drawing himself upright, and beginning to understand more clearly the pain buried in this man's heart, the Roman continued. "No matter my decision (he nodded to the villagers) these people will harm you if you remain. Understand, if you can, that I, by law, cannot send you away. But I can, as a man, say that the swan does not lie down with the carrion. The jackals see no difference between a live swan and a dead rat, and would happily tear it all apart in ignorance and hunger."

"And so I would say, as a man, for your own sake and this village's continued peace, even though it be the peace of night, I say that you must go, though it pains me that I shall not know you."

The man gazed at the distant mountains, nodding his ragged head in understanding. "I thank you for your kindness," he said, taking the Roman's hand, and gazing deeply into the man's heart as he did so. "I can see you are a patient shepherd. I wish you well with your flock."

With this parting comment he sighs. Yes, he had to leave, knowing that THIS is what he wanted to avoid. Knowing that every step would take him to a far greater danger, and a far, far more evil world. He got up, and started walking.

"Wait." the Roman called, realizing a sudden, unexplained sense of loss. "I do not even know your name!"

The man turned, his tender eyes lit with a love born of hardship and a thousand, thousand insights into the nature of man. "Yeshua," he answered. "of Nazareth." Thus he turned and left behind another town, another place. He now knew where he must go, and what he must now do. He headed West. Towards the destiny that he could no longer avoid.

Lost in the Wilderness

There was no harm in him, really.

Harry: red-eyed, loud, drunk, laughing at the smallest of things, loving his sports. Yet when he got so lost like he was right now, just abusive. "Bastards, robbed me of my life. The turds. Fucking turds. Gave my life, worked fingers to the bone..." Then he wept, and drowned ihis self pity in more booze.

Why God ever gave this man to her, she never knew. It must have been to teach her patience. He drank most of their earnings. Not always, he was once an excellent carpenter, and would still be if he could stay sober enough, for long enough. In his younger years Harry had build her this house, and it was a good house, but the booze had him for the last decade. The odd job is what paid for things now.

"I should build a yacht. I can build a fucking BOAT. Sail away, be free. Yeah, a yacht. I could build a yacht in MONTHS."

"You are not going to build a yacht, Harry." Elise said, simply, clearly, "You don't have the money, because you drank it."

"You fucking WHORE!" He shouted, and moved towards her with his fist up.

She trusted his heart, despite the lost soul wandering before her. She just held the fist. "And you aren't going to hit me, Harry. You know that as well, honey. You are just another drunk person wallowing in dreams, but I love you."

His fist drops, his voice drops, his shoulders drop. "I don't deserve you."

"You built me this house, Harry. You gave me three fine boys. You did enough to deserve some love." It was an old mantra, but it worked. Harry stared at her briefly, confused, staggered over to the couch on the porch where he sat most nights, and fell asleep right there and then.

Elise brought out the blanket, took off his boots, and levered his feet up to where they rested night after night. She took away the empty beer bottles, and put them into the now empty carton from where they came. One bottle, as it always does, is full of cigarette stubs that threaten to spread tobacco stench through the house. That one goes into a plastic bag.

As it always does.

Tomorrow he would wake and remember none of it. She sighed. She sighed and looked down at the boards she helped him nail down so many years ago.

30 years, 20 of them good ones.

It was not so bad, really.

FIGHTING FISH

Love is a slippery fish, difficult to catch, and harder to hold. You have to wait patient hours until one takes the lure of whatever your attraction might be, and then the mystery begins. You reel it in because you are hungry. The fish takes the bait because it is hungry. Every one is starving for love, or what they will call love.

Now the line is drawn tight, the bait is taken, and the dance begins. One questions remains. After you play the game, and have done rituals of the courtship, how can you know what you have brought into your life? Some fish are simple, some fish have sharp edges that will cut you, while others are downright poisonous.

It's not that this girl was dishonest. It's not that I didn't see the red lights. They were overt, obvious and glaringly well advertised. Blind Freddy would have seen them. It is just that I was so hungry, and I considered theses were like advertisements of particular zones where you should not go. Even a mine field is safe if you have the map to walk through it.

It was many, many months before I realised the simple truth, that red lights I saw were not the map to the minefield, they were simply signs to just STOP! But the sense of risk, of running the red lights, beating the minefield, winning against the odds. It is so addictive.

They say that wisdom comes in bubbles, and you have to burst something to get the message. Well it seems I had burst to plenty looking for it.

And I suppose now as I look back I did get a little wisdom. I learned this relationship was essentially a bubble making machine. She just kept creating them, I kept bursting them. She called me a prick, but it was what she wanted.

Lost friendships, lost years, lost money. These are the echoes of that crazy time. So what to do? Do you sit and count the scars, berating yourself up with the why's and wherefore's of what you might have done otherwise. You can blame yourself for missing what any other reasonable person would have seen all you like: Recrimination doesn't change that simple, honest reality which you knew and wanted: Manics were more fun in bed than ordinary girls.

It was the raw sensuality. Hard, anywhere, anytime sex. It was like a live-in hooker who would do whatever you imagined then sweep the floor and do the dishes. I thought it was heaven, despite the obvious tantrums and fury thrown around the house. Those advertisements that said: "Warning! Damaged goods".

Love would change it. Love would heal the hurt. Surely enough love and intimacy would bridge the gaping maw between the monsters of her past and the fears of her present? Then at last I understood, this particular creature didn't WANT a bridge to harmony and serenity. She lived for the rage. Just as her fury was a threat to me, my peace offering was a threat to her.

Her fury had become her life, and to diminish it meant killing her. The more kindness offered, the greater the fury grew, because to her it was a threat.

Hard to get around that. It's a real mind twister.

And the hardest part of this paradox? She had no SHOULDS. It was what I admired more than anything. I loved a woman who could live outside the box of convention. I always hated the shoulds of this world. I never liked being told what I should do, who I should be with, how I should act. But it hurt.

She was breaking down the walls of "should" inside me. Yes it hurt, but it was like hard love, a type of painful therapy. She was a visit the dentist who had run out of anaesthetic, but who pulled the teeth anyway.

So there I stood. A bird strung on a wire in a butcher shop, waiting to be dissected. I thought I had caught a fish, but the fish had caught me.

Like a wild cat she lashed out, preferring to attack than be attacked. So many red lights, so many warnings. You would have thought I got the message, and just left well enough alone. Yet as the tempest subsided, as the fury ebbed, the precious, vulnerable, beautiful creature sat there, saying "Love me?". Each time I got reeled back in. Every time I fell back into the whirlpool.

It was hardly all bad, not by a long shot. There were great moments, yet as time rolled past I came to understand that these moments were all aligned to her whims. Everything was aligned to her moods, her conditions, her wishes. My life had become a Gorgonian knot with that woman at the centre.

Woman? Women more likely. Here's the rub. As I came to understand her MPD, I realised she was many women. I even learned to see the Multiple Personalities emerge. She could be a little girl, a 16 year old temptress, then switch to an old crone, or a man hating lesbian. She could also be a hard mercenary, out to get whatever she wanted. She could also be vacant for days on end, an empty pit into which oblivion was falling.

I was going out with seven women. I had a harem hiding in a single soul.

She was many things, yet one thing she was not, the one thing she so desperately needed, was intimate. She could not trust anything or anyone.

What I came to understand is that she lived in a bubble. When you came up close, like a face coming up to a person hiding in a glass balloon, the face twisted up, it got distorted by the bubble she lived in, so that you appeared to her as a monster and clearly a threat. Someone being too close equalled danger, because you were too vulnerable, and at risk. That fragile bubble might burst! What it created was a strange, sweet monster, with a nature always shrouded in tempest, moods and convoluted notions of reality. Independence was everything, even though she was totally dependant on her moods and my wallet.

Try to to modify her opinion, redirect her behaviour to something less destructive, or demand anything, and you became the target for her venom.

Then came the passion. Manics are always driven creatures, which was great at first, but in time all that the sex meant to me was an invitation to step further into her madness.

That was when I became daddy looking after the naughty child, and the relationship altered into seamless shades of battleship grey. A ship without a rudder floating on a sea of perpetual change is not a healthy thing.

"You saved me!" she would cry. "I was a wounded dog and you took me in, fed me, looked after me, and I will love you forever."

Then, like a wounded dog, she bit me.

There was an old Indian story about a boy who finds a rattlesnake, lost, alone and freezing on a mountain. The snake says "Save me!" But the boy is not stupid. It is a rattlesnake.

As he goes to walk away, the snake calls out "Save me. You will be my friend. I will not bite you."

The boy take pity on the snake, and warms it against his body as he takes it down to a warmer place. Finally, after some hours, they arrive, and he goes to put the snake down, but it bites him! He says, "But I saved you, and you promised not to bite!"

The snake looks disdainfully at the foolish child, and says as it winds away, "You knew what I was when you picked me up."

The Giants are Friendly

We should make things crystal clear right from the start. This was a very old Giant saying, and it remains a good thing to say and do, even today. In past times many tales were told of Giants that were not true, but this saying is definitely one of their true ones.

False stories are everywhere, however. As an example: We are told that Giants are terrible Ogres who eat little children, and this is clearly false. An Ogre is an Ogre, not a Giant. Ogres are not so big and far more ugly. They are indeed an earlier race of man that went horribly wrong, a trial run if you will.

Of course, Giants stand far above humans on the evolutionary scale, and are a far older creature. Besides having opposable thumbs, and the occasional third eye, they smile which is something an Ogre never does. They also laugh, which is connected to an entirely different story about how thunder is made, but more on this later.

The point, and the simple truth is that Giants are badly misrepresented by humans, yet they remain not at all concerned about this because they are generally far too busy with their own business to be concerned about the small details that occur in those even smaller creatures we know as human.

So, the truth of the matter? In olden time when Giants openly walked the Earth, life was a Golden Age. Clear blue skies, light clouds were cotton wool pillows for angels to sleep on, and God was seen all the time. He often discussed the shape and colour of new inventions members of his creation. As an example: This is why rainbows bend! You can thank the Giants for making rainbows curved, because originally they were going to be straight up and down. But bent is a lot prettier, don't you think?

In those days, the song of the birds was the paint that the elves used to create flowers, and the scent of these flowers is what the gnomes used to craft fruit trees, turning the ends of branches on trees into bananas, and apples, and whatever fruit you could imagine.

Some things have left us. Night-bows seem to have vanished, though I think I saw one around a full moon late one autumn in New Zealand, but perhaps that was a moon-bow. Sadly, light-footed dancing cows seem to be no more. I have no idea where they might have ended up. And of course it is extremely rare to see flying horses now.

Now, to understand this story, we need to cast our imaginations back to this time, when everything was just perfect. Creation was fresh, even the dew whistled along with the birds as they awoke, and everything was brand new.

The moon watched our dreams, the winds cooled our thoughts, the tides brought us new things every day, and laughter was the common language. It had taken a long time for God to get it all sorted out. Sure, he may have gotten the rough idea up in a few days, but refining things, really getting them to work well? This took a long time.

We have already heard of the trouble with Ogres. They were just too selfish and inconsiderate to fit in with the rest of creation, and God had moved them off to the lower end of the Elf world (And you can be certain that the elves complained about their noisy parties) and replaced them with a new invention: Man. This "Human" thing seemed the ideal notion to fill out the creation God had organised. People were the very last thing he added to his little folly called Earth. Seeing that all was now finally in order, he moved onto another world. After all, that's the general business of being God, isn't it? Making new worlds.

Of course, as soon as God left, the trouble started. It was not just the door left ajar by some elves, when they were coming between their world and the human one, it was small things. Like the clouds who got tired of holding up the rainbows, and put them down so that one end rested on the ground.

Or younger clouds, who would get too excited and fill out the whole sky with rainbows, making it too bright for anyone to see where they were going. It would be a long time before sunglasses were invented, so it was a bit of a concern. Especially for the Giants, because they kept bumping their heads on new rainbows that appeared at random, and all over. There were so many rainbows that they could not even see where they were going some days.

Not such a great concern, you say? Well, think of the poor humans scattering left and right as an enormous foot came crashing down, destroying their village or even killing people. Of course the Giants did not intend to do this, but when you are really big, and you can't see where you are going, then things like this just happen.

All the people retreated into caves because it was just too dangerous to go walking. Each night the people would light fires, and wonder why God had deserted them, and left them defenceless against the horrible Giants that smashed their world to pieces. But of course, God had left the planet. Even if he did listen in occasionally, all he would hear was the shiny sound of rainbows and the clumping sound of Giants. The small cries of people were just that, small and barely noticed.

The only ones who may have been able to help were the Elves who painted the flowers, but they were busy cleaning up the mess left over by the Ogres. And anyway, with all those rainbows about flowers started to look drab and uninteresting. The Elves themselves got a little ho-de-hum about it all.

Convinced that no one cared, people started telling terrible, frightful stories about the evil Giants. They were called a punishment by God on the poor Humans. It was generally reasoned that the people must have done something terribly wrong for God to leave them in such trouble as this. This is when

---

Giants first got confused with Ogres, particularly as the odd Ogre snuck through into a human farm, when a typically careless Elf had left open the doorway between the worlds.

The tales of woe got worse and worse, and it went on in the caves at night for years and years. Each day Humans would creep about looking for some food, and each evening they would hide in the safety of a cave, telling stories about the terrible things that happened to them that day. In fact, people were generally very unhappy with just about everything. And as you know, when everyone is complaining, it just isn't a fun place to be anymore.

The children had their own world, and it was completely different from the adult version of things. The kids had fun, because even if they had to stay in a cave, they found a way to play. Life was about games, and fun sort of things, not talking about Giants. Yet every day they were warned about the evil Giants who might squash them if they did not look out.

One day some boys were talking, and they didn't believe what the adults were saying. "I think it's all poppycock and nonsense. Who has seen any Giant feet squashing anyone around here lately?" said one young fellow.

"Well I dare you to sleep outside if you are so brave then," said another.

"I will! I will walk out in the daylight and dare the Giants to stomp me!" exclaimed another. And so on, as boys do. Of course, no one went out and dared the Giants, nor did they sleep outside, yet one child called David really began to wonder.

You see, he figured that he often doesn't see the odd ant he accidentally steps on, and to the ants he would be a Giant. So maybe they really didn't know what was happening down here? He suggested this to his mother, who scoffed at the notion. He told his Uncle, who said he was a scallywag. His father had gone hunting, and David really wanted to see what he thought, but waiting around was no fun. Without telling anyone (because he would have been stopped) he decided to go see his Dad. After all, the cave was a little drab, and he wanted to see what the real world was like. And so he went outside of the caves where he and his friends spent most of their time.

He had packed a lunch, a bed roll and some supper. He also found a roll of cloth to wrap it all in, and he tied it all to his back. David was off on an adventure. No more talking, time for the wide world. And what a world it was!

In hardly any time at all David saw high trees, green forests, deep rivers and beautiful birds. He saw an Elf collecting their song and mixing it into a paint, then using this to create wonderful flowers, and he was entranced. He had no notion at all of a Giant stomping him, because it was just so lovely to be out and be free.

The Elf noticed the little Human child, and warmly waved him over to watch him make flowers. David was not so sure, but the Elf seemed friendly, so he went over to his rock shelf in the sun. The light outside in the brightness hurt his eyes, and he covered them, which made the Elf laugh. "Indeed, those rainbows have become quite the nuisance haven't they?"

David looked oddly at the Elf. He knew nothing about rainbows, but he didn't want to appear stupid, so he asked him about how he made flowers. The Elf was a very old Elf, which in Elf terms is over 1000 years. All the young ones had stopped bothering, but he liked his work of creation, so he was happy to spend some time with a youngling like this who took an interest.

"Oh, it's not so hard really. The art is in catching the Bird Song before it fades, because then you only get dull flowers." And as David watched he heard the note of a songbird float by on the breeze, and the Elf whispered up a fairy net and caught it in mid-flight. He then got it into a small bottle before it could escape, and he shook it gently. And soon the bottom of the bottle started filling with a beautiful colour.

"See," he said "nothing simpler." And the Elf then put the bottle beside some other ones, each with an amazingly bright colour in them, and he took a spatula and flicked the liquid light into the air and dusted it with pollen. This made it set into an exquisite flower, which the Elf fitted to a nearby bush.

Bees rushed to each new flower, to see what flavours they could find. And each rush of bees caught the attention of a song bird, who would sing most beautifully on seeing them. Thus the Elf had another colour for another jar.

Perhaps the Elf knew something about the Giants? David decided to ask, but just as he did, he felt a cold breeze on his back, and the Elf lept up. "Oh dear, the door has been left open AGAIN! Sorry youngling, I must go shut it before an Ogre gets out. You would not want to be in the woods with an Ogre about now, would you?"

David was sure he would not, but his chance to ask a question was now gone because the Elf took off faster than the breeze, leaving him alone in the wood with the colour jars. And of course, being a boy David had to give it a go. He took the spatula, flicked some colour up, and swept a little pollen into the air.

But he missed, the colour hit a rock (which complained loudly) the pollen hit the bees, who were expecting another flower, and they started to buzz in annoyance. Much trickier than it looked. David thought it would be best to move on and see if his Father was about.

Being out and about like this, seeing the beautiful things being created, it all made David think that he MUST be right about the Giants. After all, in a world where everything was so beautiful, why would God make such dangerous creatures to squash people? Surely there was something he could do to tell the Giants what they were doing? He made his mind up to find a high-ish spot, and to try and grab a hold of any giant feet that came along.

A nearby tree seemed to fit the bill. It was tall, and with lots of climbing branches, so up David went. He also hoped he might also see where his father was, yet after a few minutes of climbing he forgot all about everything because of the view. Down below him he started to see an endless forest, with streams and birds flying and deep blue in the distance. It all seemed impossibly high. Climbing higher, he got above the forest canopy and felt the sharp strong breeze whipping through the leaves.

It was a little scary, and then he got very scared, because a strange silvery creature appeared from nowhere, saying "Man-Thing! You do not belong here. You live in caves where I do not go. Why are you up here? Are you visiting me??"

David had no idea what this creature was, but she appeared to be a girl and very beautiful. "You are so beautiful!" he said, not really knowing what to say.

It was a air sylph, a creature of the wind, and she smiled, "I think I like you Man-thing. My relatives told me they had seen the odd one of you out and about, but that normally you lived in dark caves. If this true?"

"Well," said David, "It is true. Most of my relatives all live in caves and rarely go out. And it is dark, and it isn't beautiful like this place."

"Why would you men-things want to live in caves?" the sylph asked.

"We don't want to, it is just that the giants stomp through our lands, and they occasionally squash someone. So people hide in caves, to save themselves from the Giants."

"But you are not hiding in a cave, Man-thing. Why are you here in this tree?"

David simply said what he was doing, which was looking for a Giant to grab onto in order to ask them to step more gently.

"Well, man-thing, you obviously have never seen a giant, have you?" said the Sylph. David shook his head. The Sylph continued, "They are far too big to try and grab when they walk past, and far to fast to hold onto. I can understand why you want to speak with them, but you won't be able to jump onto them. You're just too small."

David felt very dejected. What could he do? "How do you get to meet the Giants" he asked. "I really would love to talk to one and see if this problem can be solved."

The Sylph liked David, so she decided to help. "You know, if you wait here I will see if I can catch a breeze and fly up to whisper in a passing giants ear. But you know, it's the rainbows. It is very hard for Giants at this moment."

David had no idea what the Sylph was talking about, nor any idea what it was, nor any clue as to how it was going to fly, nor the faintest clue what the rainbows had to do with anything. But the Sylph knew exactly what it was doing. Away it flew! It just leapt from the tree, and fanning wide its arms, David saw that it had threads of silk between its arms and legs. These seemed to catch the slightest of breezes. Up and away, and in a moment it was gone.

That was when David realised what it meant about the rainbows. The whole sky was a quilt of them. Rainbows were coming in from just everywhere, and clouds seemed to rushing about to put as many as they could up into the highest places they could find. He had to close his eyes, because the brightness caused them to ache.

Not having anything better to do, and believing that the odd air creature was doing something as she promised, David waited, and waited. Soon it was getting to the mid-afternoon, and David was wondering if it would be possible to sleep in a tree overnight. He took out his lunch and started eating, looking out for his father below.

Another voice chirped from behind him "Nuts". David looked about, and out of the dark hole in the tree, there was a pair of eyes looking at him. "Nuts" it said again. David didn't have any nuts. "I am sorry, whoever you are. I don't have any." He said.

"I do. I have nuts, lots of them. You want nuts?" said the eyes.

"Oh, you must be a squirrel. You have nuts you want to share?"

"Not share, swap. What are you eating?"

"Oh, this is human food. Would you like to try some?"

"Put it there," a small claw came from out of the darkness and pointed to a spot on the bough of a tree, "and I will swap a nut for it."

David took some bread from his pack, and put it where the squirrel wanted it placed, and stepped back to another bough of the tree. Sure enough, the little fellow came out, only he wasn't so little. He was fully half the size of David, and covered is a soft, velvet fur that was mottled with the browns of the forest. A few small black stripes ran down from his neck to his tail.

Squirrel, true to his word, took the morsel of bread and left an acorn in its place. Of course, David could not eat an acorn, but he was happy to share. "Do you sleep in this tree?" he asked the squirrel, as it was now standing more in the open. But Squirrel liked the bread far too much to answer him. It was gnawing into it like it was a banquet.

"More nuts?" it asked when it had finished, obviously wanting more.

"Well, I can't really eat acorns like you can, but I will swap you some more Human Food if you can show me a safe place to sleep." David bargained. He realised that it was getting too late to get back to his cave, and that he needed to wait here to see if any giants showed up.

Squirrel simply pointed to another hole in the tree, a little higher up. David smiled, it was a good bargain for the little fellow, but equally good for him. So he put down a larger piece of bread, and climbed up to the hole. Surprisingly, it was quite large enough for him to settle into and, putting down some bedding, he curled up to wait to see what would happen.

He must have been far more tired then he imagined, for within moments he was fast asleep, and dreaming of a strange world where dragons flew and ice coated the ground. When his eyes opened it was dark outside, and though David had seen stars, never had he seen stars like this.

Up here above the canopy, they seemed so close. He felt he could reach out and touch the night itself. The cool air was very sharp outside his little sleep spot, but he dare not go out because he could not see. The boughs of the tree were just shadows. What an amazingly high cave he had found up in a tree!

For the first time, it struck him that he had told no one that he had left. Oh dear, he thought, I will be in trouble tomorrow. His mother will be fretting, and his father may even be back. Well, there was nothing for it now but to wait and see what tomorrow brings. David closed his eyes, drinking in the splendour of the night with his ears and nose, feeling it tingle on his skin, and he slept a deep, deep sleep.

He awoke in the morning to the sound of a hum that vibrated the leaves of his tree. The wind had picked up, and was sweeping through the air like a knife, swaying the tree itself. Squirrel popped his head up to say good morning, asking for more bread. Well, thought David, I will be heading home soon, so he may as well share breakfast with me. So he showed the last bread roll to the Squirrel and broke it into half.

Squirrel was more confident now he had a Human Thing that slept like a proper animal, not stuck in some dingy cave, and he was entirely talkative. In fact, he nattered on non-stop. "Do you like the tree? I love it. I always come back here. It's my home you know. You can live here as well if you like, you like it here to? I do. I like it a lot." And so he went for quite some time.

Finally Squirrel asked, "What were you talking to the Sylph about?"

"The what?" questioned David.

"The air sylph you were talking to yesterday. They never stop and talk to me, so what did she want?"

"Oh," said David. "Well I wanted to know about Giants and the Sylph said it would go find one and bring it here, or at least I think that is what she meant. I am not sure, so I was waiting to find out."

"Giants! Giants you say? You want to meet a giant?" the squirrel seemed amazed. "My grandmother met a giant once, a long time ago. I have never seen one, though I hear them occasionally galumphing about. My Grandmother said only one thing about them, you know. Only one thing."

David presumed he was meant to ask what that was, so he did.

"The Giants are friendly" the squirrel finished, almost. "You wouldn't imagine it, and I don't suppose it's true, but that's what grand mama said, and she never lies, so that what she believes, but I can't say for certain its true."

"I find that big things are dangerous and want to eat me. So I don't want to meet a giant and then find out it isn't friendly. Oh no, and anyway, they probably wouldn't even see me, let alone stop and talk. But I do like it when they go past, because they knock a lot of nuts out of the trees, yes they do. Lots of nuts... Nuts... Yes... Nuts..."

Squirrel disappeared. Obviously the importance of gathering nuts was higher than chatting with a human who had run out of bread. Then it popped back, "Bread, that is what you call it? I will always swap you nuts for bread."

This time it was really gone. Its tail bobbed through the branches, and in a flash it was not to be seen as it dashed off from tree to tree on its search for food. However, the message had a strong impact on David. It seemed to make sense, that just as he meant no harm to the ants, the giants meant no harm to people. Then perhaps they really were friendly? It could be just as he suspected, that they just didn't notice small things.

Isn't it interesting how understanding grows when we look at things from a new angle? His curiosity to know the real story was getting much stronger, and he wondered if the Sylph was able to find a giant, and if the giant would come, and what the giant might say, and what would HE say?

David needed his curiosity in the next moment, he needed everything he could muster to keep him in his spot in the tree, for in the distance he heard the crashing sound of what he knew had to be a Giant!

A Meeting in the Clouds

Closer and closer it came, and for the first time David was able to grasp just how stupendously huge the Giants really were. This one had to stoop just to get under the clouds, and it seems he was looking for something. David could feel the rumble of the earth as it shook under the weight of the huge being, yet at the same time, it seemed to be stepping lightly, carefully.

"The Giants are friendly" he kept saying to himself, nervously, over and over. His heart was racing, his mouth was dry, and his anxiety was starting to take over. He wanted to creep back into his hole and hide, but somehow he found the bravery to stand in the open. Then without warning, a huge foot crashed near his tree, breaking branches and shaking the trunk so strongly that David had to hold on for dear life.

"HELP!" he cried out to no one.

Suddenly it all stopped. A deep voice called from the heavens. "Is this the little human child the sylph told me to come and see?" it asked.

David was speechless! The Sylph really had done it, it had whispered in the ear of a giant, and here it was! It had come all this way just to see him. "Yes" he called out. "I am that child!"

An enormous eye came down from the sky, and squinted. "My, but you are such a tiny thing." A voice said, filling the air with rumbling. "Hold on, I will bring you up where it is more comfortable for me to talk to you." And with this, a huge pair of fingers grabbed the entire tree and plucked it up into the air.

Up, up, up it went, with David clinging on for dear life. Higher and higher. The horizon was far below as the cold high air bit into David's hands. But he dare not let go. Instead he leapt into the hollow where he had slept the night, and finally felt a small degree of safety.

Still higher he went, above the forest, above the world, until he started to see clouds speaking to each other as they carried their rainbows about. Finally, away up so high that he dare not look down, David came face to face with the Giant. "There" it said, "Now I can see you little Human. What is it that you wanted to ask the Giants?"

What could he say? David said the truth "Mr Giant, I am sure you don't realise it, but your great feet and those of your brothers are squashing we humans whenever you walk about. We are all living in caves, scared of being killed by your boots. Is there anyway that you look where you are going?"

"It's those foolish rainbow hanging clouds," said the Giant matter of factly. "They got this job with the rainbows, and they have gone too far, far too far. None of us can see where we are going anymore, because the whole sky is filled with rainbows. But what can we do about it? It's just terrible, doublely triplely terrible now that I know we are squashing Gods creatures." And with this a huge tear welled up in the giants eye, and falling down David could see it crashing down onto the ground. "Oh my goodness!" he said to himself.

He had no idea that Giants were so sensitive. "Well," David said. "It's not that so many people get squashed, it is just that everyone lives in a cave and is afraid to walk in the woods."

"Oh my double goodness," the Giant exclaimed. "This is even WORSE. This is just the most terrible thing I have ever heard, and now I am afraid to take even one step. It's those CLOUDS I tell you, and I just don't know what we can do about this!"

"Well, I don't suppose you could get Gods attention, could you Mr Giant?" David suggested. "After all, we are so small I don't think he can hear us. Maybe if you call out he might hear, and can sort this all out?"

"Well little one. I can try, but God is off making another world just at the moment. But I will try." and with this, the giant cupped one hand to his enormous mouth, and called out to the heavens. "GO-O-O-O-D! Are you there God? Oh Goooooooooddddd!"

His voice shook the very moisture from the air. All the clouds were so shaken they lost all their rain, and completely forgot about holding up the rainbows, which they dropped. Suddenly all the rainbows fell from their places and as they fell they shattered into snowflakes, causing the whole of the land below to become covered in a blanket of multi-coloured winter.

"Goooooooood?" called out the Giant, creating the first roar of thunder.

Fortunately, just as the Giant called out, God had put the finishing touches to a particularly clever new idea he had, a thing he called a mountain and he just happened to hear his name being called from the last world he had been working on. So he opened his eyes in the direction of the call, and saw the Giant holding one of his Human children. "How odd," thought God.

"Well, we are in luck, little one. It seems that God has heard and is here." said the Giant.

David was not so sure. He could see nothing, not that he knew what a God looked like, but he saw nothing at all. "Are you sure, Mr Giant. Are you certain that God heard you? I can't see him anywhere."

"Oh little one. You never SEE God. You can only FEEL him. Can you feel that big sense of being "right here" in your heart? Can you feel that complete sense of everything being in the right place at the right time?"

Truth to tell, this is what David felt. Everything seemed perfect, even the rainbows falling, the clouds shaking, the incredible height he was at. It all just seemed perfect. "Yes, I can feel this. Is this God?"

"Yes," said the Giant. "He is present within your heart. Now just speak your heart, and your heart will hear."

David spoke about everything his family had been through, what they feared, what the problem was, and how he knew the Giants didn't mean to be hurtful, but please: Can we do something to make the world safer for all?

Now, just as the Giant had promised, God WAS listening, and it was quite a puzzle for him. "Obviously," thought God, "The clouds have gotten a little enthusiastic with the rainbows. But what to do?" This is more difficult than it seems, because God never wants to restrict even the smallest thing in his creation from doing what is natural for them to do. I mean this is the whole point of creation, that it does what it does. But it was very clear that a little extra organisation was needed on this world.

So God decided he needed to set up rules for the clouds and the weather. There were to be so many sunny days, so many cloudy ones. So much rain, and sadly he had to put a rule on the favourite of his, the rainbows. They were only allowed out after rain, and at no other time.

Of course, this did not solve the problem of the little people hiding in caves. So God decided to make his giants invisible, so that they could not be seen, thus not scare the people. Of course, he also had to solve the problem of their rather large feet, so in a wink he waved for areas of the land to rise up, and he created his latest fashion all over the earth, a thing we now call the mountain ranges. These were the new walkways for his giants. The solution was so simple: God made them so high that people were not able to live there.

Of course, for David things looked rather shocking. Suddenly instead of a giant before him, he was suspended high above the clouds by nothing. His tree just floated there in space. The Giant had vanished right before his eyes! In the distance he saw whole sections of land rising up, and with the earth growling like a tiger, it formed huge hills.

Down David went. Just as quickly as he had rushed up towards the heavens, now he was drawn down, down, down to the ground yet again. He must have passed out, because he remembered nothing of how he got to be back on the earth until he woke up in his special little hidey hole in the tree.

Was it all a dream? Then he looked down, and saw all around this amazing rainbow coloured snow. Wonderful! It had really happened, he had really met one of the Giants, and just as the Squirrel had said: The Giants WERE Friendly.

Of course, no one believed his tale, and it took many years for his family to move out of the caves. But as time went past, the talk of Giants squashing people faded away, and the people started to live out in the open once more.

Naturally, the odd Ogre still escaped through some door left open by a lazy Elf, and this is how Ogres got turned into Giants in the Human stories.

But the real message was a very simple one. Whenever David was afraid of anything, he always remembered his journey to the wilderness, his meeting with a friendly Giant. Because of this he could now believe that if he listened closely to his heart, there he might ask God for an answer.

Slow Train Comin

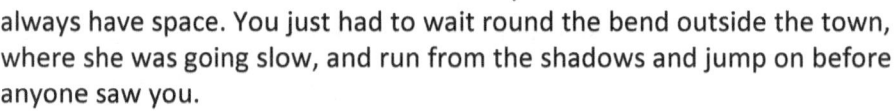

Peter looks up. The old familiar whistle, the solid ker-chunka-tuck-chucka vibration through the ground meant Old Familiar was pulling into the station. "Come on Simple Simon," he says, "this is our ride."

The two hobos wait in the shadows, looking for the open door of a goods carriage. No one much minds a hobo, but in days past, because of the violence and drunkenness, it meant carriages became more closely watched. But trains like Old Familiar on these back tracks always seemed to always have space. You just had to wait round the bend outside the town, where she was going slow, and run from the shadows and jump on before anyone saw you.

These back ways saw few passengers since the automobile had come along, and this old steam train was kept in service by the collier more because the company was too tight to invest in diesel than any sense of romance. It was depression era middle America, and what little money there was flowed towards the richer fields of the Eastern and Western states.

Simple Simon was slow, but Peter encouraged him. "Just take the first step Simon, get the feet going and the body will follow." Simon obeyed, as always. He stumbled at first, but then got his speed up. Soon they are sitting in an open flattop, smelling the coal steam mingling with nature. "Where to now, Simon? Where to now." Peter asks his silent friend, who just smiles. A lamb following it's mother.

"Next town, next life." says Peter, answering himself.

They sit there for a while, and high in the sky Peter sees an eagle. "Simon, use your stuff and talk to that eagle. Tell it to circle round the other way."

Simon smiles. He loves these games. He nods, then looks with an intent focus up at the bird, and with just his mind he sees the eagle turn the other way. He holds the picture, looking with total focus, and waits.

They both laugh as the eagle changes direction, and spirals the opposite way in the sky. Peter smiles. "You see, Simon? Just a little focus can go a long way. But let's test you on some harder stuff. See the diesel train coming up to our rear, you know it's going to whistle this old rattler to the siding, and when trains stop they check for hobos like us. Now we don't want that do we?" Simon looks very concerned, and shakes his head.

"Well we got to use that gift of yours to help ourselves here. We got to focus on stopping that big old train. You got that?" Simon looks very unsure.

"Yeppers, it is a big train alrighty but don't let that put you off. Big things are made of lots of little things. All we have to do is focus on a little thing to stop and we can make the big thing scratch itself and get confused. Now what I want you to do is to focus on the back carriage, the very back one, you got that?"

Simon nods. "And you got to see those back wheel a'lockin up. You got that, just see those back wheels all sparkin' up. Just a single wheel a sparkin' up. That'll cause 'em to stop and sort out the brakes. Just one wheel's enough. There Simon, you can do that, just one wheel."

Simon looks worried, but he focuses. "Just one wheel" Peter encourages, "Just one wheel". Intent concentration, beads of sweat, and forced breathing as Peter says to him over and over "Just one wheel, just one wheel"

And then there is a shower of sparks from the rear of the approaching train, and true to his promise, the train is flagged to a stop so the problem can be inspected. Peter says "You see, just one wheel and the whole damn train stops to see what's wrong, and we carry on." Simon smiles broadly.

"Remember Simon, it's always the little things. Taking the first step, one little thing done right. This is what moves us through and stops the heeby jeebies. Simon shuddered. He hated the Heebie Jeebies. It was an evil thing that came whenever you doubted yourself, a thing that got under your skin made you fearful. "You'll get past the heebie jeebies Simon, a step at a time, a day at a time," says Peter encouragingly

For now the slow rattle of the carriages was like a mother's arms, and Simon slipped off to sleep knowing he had his friend Peter to look after him.

The Next Day

When he woke, Simon was not surprised to find himself at the next town. It was always this way, ever since he had met Peter, his friend and protector. He got so dopey when he fell asleep that he never remembered waking up. Peter said he just had to talk to him, and he'd sleep walk him off the train and into some back spot where Hobo signs said it was safe.

Simon was very simple. He didn't remember anything much of the past, and had no notion of what the future was, let alone ask any questions about it. He was content to just go with the wind and the rail and see where things went. Peter was there to look after him.

"Time we did something to earn some breakfast young man" Peter said. Simon got up. Peter always found something for them to do that gave them food or something that made life better. "We got to use those powers of yours, Simon. We got to find someone who needs some help, and you can help them, and we can have some supper, yes?" Simon nods in agreement.

As they get to walk there is a scream from a house nearby, a woman screaming. "Well that sounds like someone is calling for us!" says Peter delightedly. And they walk up to the house finding the door wide open and a woman whimpering in fear "No, not the children! Don't hurt the children."

Simon glows red with anger as he sees a man with a large stick. He has beaten the woman, and, drunk and stupid he is about to set onto his kids. Peter holds him on the shoulder, "Little things Simon. Little things to stop the big things. Use your power to help everyone, not to harm anyone."

Simon is puzzled. He wanted to make that stick turn and hit the man, hit him till he bled, but instead he thought more. He thought hard, and as the man went to bring the stick down on the youngest child, he had an idea. All this anger, all this hate. It had to come from somewhere.

And like magic the door opened, and he saw that man being beaten by his own drunken father as a child, and his mother to one side, screaming like this one here. That man had a mother, that man once had someone who wanted to protect him. What if he spoke to his mother?

Then using the peculiar ability Simon had, he looked through the veil of reality and asked for the man's mother. She came forward, weeping like the woman before him, and looked the man in the eye as she stepped right in front of the falling cane.

The man freezes in place. He can't believe his mother, long dead is before him. He can't hit his mother, she was the only one who ever loved him. He remembers how his father used to beat him, for no reason, how his mother used to cry like his wife in the corner. He remembers the hate, the fear, the helplessness. And he weeps, and realises he has become his father. He stands there shaking, still holding the weapon, weeping like the child he once was.

He throws it down, "I am so sorry" is all he can say as he staggers in drunken stupor out the door, not even seeing Simon or Peter.

Then the sound Simon always feared, Mr Heebie Jeebie calls from the background, "Damn you gone done it again you little whimp! He was MINE, and you done making MY people change like that!"

Simon couldn't help himself, he ran. He ran because some deep chord of fear took control in the place where reason no longer spoke. He ran and hid and shook in fear. Peter eventually caught up with him. Peter could always find him, and thankfully he has a basket of food. "There you are. You done panicked again Simon, just because ole Heebie Jeebie got to you ." Peter laughs, and rolls out some food.

"That woman was so grateful she gave us a virtual banquet I tell you, so eat up, you earned it. You did real good there. You did REAL good."

Simon had curled up in a ball behind a rundown ironworks, noted mostly for the lack of activity. The whole town had a sense of silence, the silence of people waiting for something to happen. He slowly unwound, and started to eat. Peter looked out at the grey world around him."It's hard for people right now, real hard. No money, no prospects. People turn and get angry at the world, but the world's so big they can't beat it. So they turn inside and just get angry at everything they see."

Simon loved listening to Peter talk. He loved his confidence, the thing he had none of. "You know, the Heebie Jeebie Man is not as real as you think, Simon. It is real for you, I know that, but it's not as real as you believe. It's like that big train though, you got to figure some small thing to stop it running you down like it does."

"But when a bull is running at you in a field, all you can think of is getting out of the way. I understand that. I understand completely. But one day you got to trip that bull up, you hear me? One day, you gonna trip that bull up."

"Now I found a place for us to sleep and stay the night, so let's get packin' and we see what tomorrow brings, you hear me Simon? You hear me?"

Simon never spoke. He was not sure if he could, or more, if he even wanted to. He just nodded. Thank God he had Peter.

The Second Day, and the next, and the ones after that.

Each day they made their way to the station and caught a train to somewhere, and all through each day Peter's comforting voice was a beacon shining a way out of the confusion where Simon lived.

Each day they walked into some situation where Simon's special gift could help someone. Simon could remember things a little now. He started to go over what he had done, and started to understand his purpose just a little.

The man who was about to be poisoned by his business partner. The man had been in Europe raising money for his railway project, and had just returned home. Peter and he has walked in as he was about to have a whiskey after work and begin to go through the financial records of his partnership. If he had read more than a few pages, the man would have seen the theft and deceitful practices that had happened in his journey away, and the partner knowing his habits had ensured that he never lived long enough to understand.

Peter had puzzled. It was easy enough to remove the poison from the whiskey, but he saw a new future open, where the man became enraged with what he found, and had killed the partner inadvertently in a brawl. Thus a good man went to jail and a good business went to ruin, with all the families it supported suffering as the consequence. Peter had helped him. Pointing out a various futures. Asking what seemed to be a solution.

You cannot ask a dishonest man to be honest, or a proud man to become humble. Change, real change has to come as a want from inside. Simon had a deep sense that the sin of the partners greed was in some way matched by the sin of the good man's pride. Was one any better or worse than the other? Each were trailing behind the effects of their own circumstances.

Then he realised that instead of the whiskey, the financial records and the conflict that flowed from these, both men could be united in the one thing they both loved: Nature. So he opened a door where both men could step through, to a beautiful lake with the moon shining softly down.

He made it so when the man got back, the moon was shining through an open door, and it was so beautiful he called his partner out to share it.

And the two partners, for the first time in year, spoke together and shared their love of the wilderness in a way that united them. There our thief has a moment of epiphany; that there was something greater than himself, a greater purpose to serve, and he confessed to the good man of his wrongdoing.

He begged his forgiveness and promised to pay back the monies. He explained it was gambling, an evil that had taken hold of him, but one which he would conquer. The Good Man was struck by his partners sincerity, and revealed that the small amount of funds he was in debt for was nothing compared to the funds he had raised in Europe. He admitted to having had his doubts about his partner, which is why he never spoke of his success till that moment.

And so from the sorry state of lies, theft and overweaning pride, a new partnership was born, and many families had gainful employment in the construction of a new railroad.

Peter had said he was particularly proud of Simon the way he had figured out a solution. Simon still heard the jabbering of the Heebie Jeebie Man in the background, but of recent times it stayed away from direct confrontation. Peter had said it was because there was no room for the Heebie Jeebie. Simon knew with all his heart that he had done the right thing, and fears could not control him.

But things were not always so perfect. Many, many days before they had visited the plantation of a wealthy man. His wife had been unfaithful to him, with an army officer, and the man was furious. He had given her everything, and to be humiliated like this was beyond his ability to contain the rage to murder her.

A simple lock on a solid wooden door was the solution. Maybe not the best, but it was all Simon could think of at the time. He locked her in and away from the insane, vengeful husband. The army man, seeing his career at risk, simply petitioned his higher officer to be moved to a different posting.

Odd that it was the Civil War, but like all his moments, these things came and passed through, like water running down a stream.

He didn't think that was a good solution, but Peter had simply said "There are times when understanding and compassion just cannot happen until wounds are healed. You created a distance that allowed the wounds to heal."

But the Heebie Jeebie man was cruel and taunted him, and laughed about that. Simon suffered many days of pain, listening to the jeers echoing from that evil man. And he began to wonder why he could change everything else, but not this.

He had the gift. Simon knew he had the gift now. Peter saw it and had kept showing him ways to use it, ways to help others, yet he could not seem to help himself. Perhaps he wasn't meant to.

Yet, as each stage of the journey was met with a more complete answer, a better solution, the less power the Heebie Jeebie Man seemed to hold over him.

So many days, so many people suffering the consequences of fate. In every stage of the journey Simon began to see the simplicity, a solution within our trials. The reason we all suffered was because we failed to understand the whole. When you understood the greater picture, the small pieces of pain and suffering were just part of the colour that made the thing complete. You just had to get people to open their hearts to the whole picture, to see outside of the small world of their own making, and you could set them free.

Simon knew that somehow this was the story of the Heebie Jeebie Man as well. Simon just needed to understand WHY he was part of the picture.

After Time Stood Still

It is difficult to understand how moments flow together when your mind is chained to the harsh rhythm of a clock, but as the train rattled its way through the forest, moments flowing to moments seemed the most natural and easy thing. They had been travelling for months, from town to town, state to state, season to season, and even, as it seemed, across the years themselves.

Simon felt a deep lightness enter his heart as the cool air from the mountains took away the heat of the lowlands. It was a sense of purpose, despite his natural confusion, he had a sense of belonging not to a place, but to a way of life. Yet against this sweet freedom a disturbing sense kept coming to him that day. It was not the Heebie Jeebie Man, but a deeper sense that he was missing something. Peter, who always seemed to have answers, today said nothing. Today Peter himself seemed weighed down with a silence.

"We are coming to a place you will recognise, Simon. Now, I know that you don't really see anything but each moment, but we are coming to a place where things will seem different." Peter said solemnly. He paused, looked at the dumbfounded creature before him, and wondered: *was it time?* They had been travelling the byways for so long now. Simon had been learning to control and focus his mind, and use his gift to help others.

But as much as he had his doubts, as much as he wondered if his friend was ready, the train itself took the journey to where they needed to go, and it was not for him to question. "We are almost there, but you need to understand the place we are going to is not like where we have been. We are travelling to your past today, Simon. We are travelling to a place you left long ago. Just remember if you can, that even though it is the past, it is still like the train, just that one wheel you can stop turning can stop the whole damn thing."

Simon went to speak. It seemed to him that he had nothing to say, and yet some part of him wanted to speak for the first time in his living memory. But he had nothing to say, so he just sat there, looking out from the carriage, feeling the chatter of the wheels on the tracks.

The train pulled up at a homestead, not a station. The place was deserted. Simon felt an uncomfortable sense but Peter got off, and signalled for him to do so.

Dead bodies littered the ground. The man, his wife, his children, all dead. The blood, freshly spilled, soaked into the dry soil. Was it Indians? No, in the distance he could see white men riding away, the rifles still hot with the bullets they fired.

The ghost of the man and his wife saw him, and said "You know why this happened. You know that you could have changed things. Why didn't you?" Simon was shocked. Only Peter and the Heebie Jeebie Man ever spoke to him directly. He didn't know what to say. His mind followed the riders as they made their way back to town, as they went to the rich man who paid them the blood money.

He watched as the man grew furious, and shouted at the men. He abused them, and decried their stupidity. They were only supposed to push things over, burn a barn, push the settlers off. Murder was another matter. The men say they had to. The man had pulled a rifle and was shooting at them, and so was his wife. It was self defence.

And the CHILDREN? Did the children shoot at them?

The men shuffle. Their habit was to leave no witnesses. They look at each other, and at the rich man before them. And now they realise, there is still one witness left.

They made it look like a robbery, the dead man forced to hand over the numbers to the safe before they shot him through the muted blanket, and away they rode. They had nothing but contempt for the rich man and the stupid farmer. You don't employ men like themselves and not expect to bear the consequences.

But Simon did not understand. He had no power to change this. He went to change things, but nothing happened.

It was so simple. The farmer had just wanted to protect his land. The Rich man wanted to buy it because it backed onto gold fields he wanted sole access to, and he was not telling anyone WHY he needed that property.

Rich man versus poor man. Rich man attitude was one of superiority. He made the poor one an offer for double its worth, and the fool would not sell. Well, then his life was to be made uncomfortable until he decided it was in his best interest to move on. But to the farmer, the land was gold beyond price. He loved the mountains behind, he loved the river it sat upon, he loved the trees and animals that ran wild there. He was happy, and money was never his goal.

He thought the rich man an utter fool for wanting to pay too much. He knew the lands value, after all, he had worked for years to afford it. But here he had friends, neighbours who loved his family, and he had set into this soil roots that were his own. Nothing would move him, or his wife.

Rich man sends thugs to rough up poor man, to show him who is boss. Poor man had seen gunslingers before, he knew what they were doing, so he reached for his gun, as had his wife from the homestead behind him.

No one realised how the laugher of the Heebie Jeebie Man can drive men to insane acts. But there was the face clearly now. Simon saw it like it was day itself. The man running this gang of murderers was none other than the one he most feared.

Heebie Jeebie Man looked at him, laughing, and says, "You see coward! You see now?"

Simon fell into shock. The words stabbed his heart, and he collapsed to the ground. Peter, saying nothing, just picked him up and carried him back to the train. He put him down on the open rattler, and let the slow beating rhythm of the train lull his friend to sleep. Simon, in a semi-conscious state, knew the journey was coming to an end. He heard the wheel slow, the sound of water, and heard the quiet, keen whistling of the wind as it cut through the arctic pines on the ridge in the distance. He felt deaths cold embrace.

He opened his eyes to see Peter looking at him, saying nothing. The train had come to a dead stop in the middle of a lake tinged with ice. Bitter chill nipped at his heart, and all that was warm and caring seemed to have been taken away. It was desolate, alone and unforgiving.

Finally words came to Simon's long silent mouth. "What was that all about?"

Peter is very serious, very clear. "You remember our journey, Simon? You remember all the places we have been, the things we have done?" He nods.

"Good. Do you also remember that no matter how difficult the situation we faced together, no matter how terrible the consequences, there was always another way? You remember how there is ALWAYS another way we can find that makes life better for all?"

Simon can say nothing, but his mind goes back over the journey, and the incredible sense of worthiness he felt finding the way to help others find a better way.

"Simon, I am your guardian angel, and your life came to an end at the hands of those gunmen you hired to sort out the poor farmer and his family." Peter paused to let this soak in. "You remember how people say how their whole life flashes before their eyes? Well, that's a little of what's been a happenin' here with us.

"All those stories we lived through? In some way they came from inside you. You are the one who brought yourself to them, to sort out some deep puzzle inside yourself before we went onto to the judgement. And you done real good, Simon, you done real good.

"Now, soon we will have to go to the place where you will pay for what you have done. I won't be with you there, and must stay away until you have learned the lesson. But try to remember all these past journeys we have taken. All of these have been to show you that there is always another path we can take. But only if we remain aware of the greater picture.

"Now this place you will be sent to is called Hell. It hurts in ways that will make your Heebie Jeebie Man seem nothing, but I want you to understand, it is not eternal as some try to say. It may seem that way, but it is not.

"All these places you visited. All of these are like reflections from your own past. Every little piece is like a lifetime you lived where you failed to act in a way that was good for all. Selfish thinking and cruel acts are ruled by our fears, not by our hearts. It is our fears that bring us to hell, Simon, always our fears.

Peter stood up, and with his hand commanded Simon to rise as well. "Now Simon, here is the most amazing part of it all. This is the reward for the good things. All of this we have done has been to help you do one single thing: Open your Heart. So let's take all we have gained from our travels, and just do it!

"Let your heart open."

Simon went to say that he couldn't. He felt intense guilt for what he had down, and yet he also felt this deep seed take root. The good he had done had somehow set roots into his inner soil, just like the poor farmer and his wife. But Peter's words were not a request, they were a command. Simon felt a power flowing into him, a power of sincerity, warmth and clarity.

He felt it flow down into him from the eyes of the angel, through his being, down to the tips of his fingers and toe. And then it released outwards, taking all his fear and suffering, all his misery and doubt, and with this release his heart opened. And the freedom! He felt the current of life itself take him up to the heavens, and he soared like the eagle. High into the sky he flew, and beside him, with magnificent wings of light, flew his friend Peter. Finally Simon can speak freely, but the only words he wants to say are, "I am Free!"

He had never known such freedom, such a sense of being. It was intense, brilliant and utterly entrancing. It was all of eternity wrapped up in a brilliant moment of NOW.

Then it all stopped. The wings compressed back into his heart. The freedom stopped while the pain and memory of his past arose once again. Where had that freedom gone? Simon was back on the train now, back on the desolate lake, the end of the line. Peter looked sorrowfully at him, saying "That was Heaven, Simon. You had to experience that to realise just how much this is Hell. Alone, utterly alone, and locked up inside yourself.

"Now you have to find your way out."

Rock-a-bye baby, from the treetop. And down comes baby, cradle and all. And he falls, he falls through this reality into an emptiness beyond comprehension.

The Return

Simon Petersen woke in a profuse sweat. He shook from head to foot as a reaction. Such a nightmare that was, going to hell. Already the details were vague as he struggled to consciousness, but he clearly remembered something about some angel sending him to hell.

He shuddered, not being a religious man, but wondering what that was about. He went to his bathroom, washed his hair and face, rubbed some Epsom salts into his gums, and chewed a mint to freshen up the breath, dressed, and went down to his office. His secretary had coffee brewed and he sat to drink.

"Good Morning Mr Petersen." she said cheerily. As always he just grunted. And as always, first order of business every day was to check his diary. Only one thing there ... *1:00pm: A meeting with H Jeebus. Instructions on how to deal with Harry Palmer.*

Something was wrong with this, but he couldn't place it. He had his doubts about this man. Something seemed not right, he was just too weird, too untrustworthy.

Something else niggled the back of his mind. The fool farmer had no idea of the worth of what he was sitting in front of with the ONLY damn access beyond spending a year cutting through the mountains behind him. WHY didn't he take the offer? The farm itself had no value to him. He only wanted the access to the gold behind it, but he wanted this fact as secret as it could be, for as long as possible. There had to be something to get these people to stand aside, but for the life of him, he did not see what.

Then on impulse he did something he never did. He turned to his secretary Miss Peta Frobisher, strange name for a girl, Peta, and asked her. "Miss Frobisher, you know I want the Palmer farm, you know he won't sell. Have you ANY idea what I can do to get him to sell up?"

She seemed a little shocked that her boss would ask a mere woman's opinion, but she smiled. "Mr Petersen, I know he will never sell, not willingly. It's more than a farm to him, more than soil and rocks.

"I was speaking to his wife just last week when they came in to talk to you about your offer. He's from a broken home, where his drunken father used to beat him for no good reason, and she said to me that she herself used to live in daily fear of her life. But then a miracle happened! One that stopped her husband being a drunk and abusing her. Apparently his mother came to him from the grave and stopped him beating his children, and that's something more powerful than any fear of God from a preacher. He stopped the booze, he stopped beating her, and they saved up. They both worked for three years and saved every penny to buy that farm you so badly want.

"They got to that farm, and by this time he had changed completely. He had become a GOOD man, and as his wife said, even she was surprised at the amount of good in him.

"That farm represents his salvation before God, Mr Petersen. You will never be able to offer him money enough, not three times it's worth, not four times. You would have to kill him and his family to move them off there.

A shudder went down his back. There was something familiar in all of this. That was the moment Simon Petersen stopped. He had never been stopped. He always got his way. "So you say there is no way I can get that farm?"

Miss Frobisher decided that spades needed to be called spades. "Mr Petersen, everyone knows you want the farm for some reason. You are a smart, clever man, and there is a reason for everything you do. No one knows WHY you want that land, but everyone knows there is a reason for it.

"But the fact is, Mr and Mrs Palmer will NEVER sell. Not ever, not for any money or any reason. If you want something connected to that land, you are going to have to share WHY you want it, and share a little of what you hope to get from it."

Simon Petersen looked at his secretary with new respect. Few men could be so plain speaking to him, and yet this little woman made perfect sense. He stopped, and he thought, and he wondered what he might do.

Finally, after many minutes of silence, he said, "Do you think that the education of his children, in fine schools with enough money to be well dressed, and well fed, might persuade Mr Palmer and his wife that I might have unimpeded access through his property?"

Miss Frobisher almost blushed "I do believe you are the smartest man in this entire valley, Mr Petersen, because that is the only thing Mr and Mrs Palmer are working for, a better life for their children. I do believe they will be listening hard to your offer."

"Cancel that one pm appointment, Mrs Frobisher. Contact the blacksmith and organise me a horse. I believe, since the Palmers were so kind as to visit me, that I owe them a return favour. Oh, and get a me a dress that Mrs Palmer might like from the haberdasher, some toys for the children, and I do believe that Mr Palmer could use some new tools, maybe a brand new axe."

That afternoon, with the sun beating down and a light breeze cutting through the trees, Simon Petersen felt a change happen, a change deep down inside his heart. There was a brightness to the air, and a lightness within. Things went back to a time long before paperwork and bank balances, to himself as a child, fishing from a river, perfectly content.

He remembered when he realised he had the gift, the gift of making things happen. He could just focus, and things seemed to just take the shape he desired. That's what frustrated him so much about the Palmers. They were immune to his power. Now he felt grateful that they were.

Riding out on a horse to the Palmer Homestead, carrying the things he knew would bring a smile to so many faces, Mr Petersen felt something he had not felt in a long time ... Real Freedom.

Dedicated to Bill Flavell
(A genuine Hobo with
the heart of an angel)

We Be Brothers, or We Be Others

The Sad, Sad Tale of the Tiger who Loved

Tiger prowled in the dark, dangerous forest. He had lived and hunted here for so long that he no longer had any idea of time, nor when he had first arrived. Yet he certainly remembered the taste of the soft deer and the sweet, tender little rabbits that found their way to his belly.

Indeed, all the creatures of the forest feared and respected the great hunter, and bowed low as soon as they saw him. Not out of respect, but in the hope he wouldn't see them. Tiger accepted this with resignation. He was quite used to being alone, and he could hardly expect to make friends with someone he may choose to eat the in the coming day. So it came to be that the only passing companionship the Tiger knew were other dangerous creatures of the forest.

But snakes and leopards do not make pleasant company. Leopards are so vain, and call out from a distance about how many animals they killed that day, and snakes are so preoccupied with themselves that any conversation is largely bent around their own concerns.

The arrogant cheetah was the preferred choice. Tiger knew he acted so vain because Cheetah was constantly aware of how much larger his cousin was to himself. Being the far more powerful of the two, he could accept the frailty and insecurity of his cousin, though it was still annoying.

Elephants could be good company, but they were always moving on and they were naturally cautious of Tigers wanting conversation. In most animal's experience, a big cat is chatting to you because of what he might get, which is usually yourself!

Competition, thought Tiger as he padded through the brush, competition is the law of this jungle. He personally was not so interested in being better than another, as he had nothing to prove. All he wanted to do was eat his fill, and Tiger had little need for anything else. After all, Tiger's as a breed are exceptionally lazy. The sun would often shine down as he slept in peace, totally relaxed, and entirely comfortable in his own skin.

And so it was that Tiger spent most of his time alone, and was quite content. One day things changed, however. He had gone outside of his normal territory following the scent of some rabbit, and something strange happened to him. Perhaps it was the new territory, perhaps something in the light, but Tiger felt an extraordinary warmth and openness in his heart. He quite lost sense of time, and in a break in the forest he walked into a patch of brilliant sunshine.

There were sweet smelling flowers, songbirds singing, a gentle breeze blowing and a stream flowing through a peaceful meadow. There was nothing of his normal world of shadowy underbrush, high trees and permanent shadow here. And it felt good. He lost his sense of hunger, and his desire to prowl any further. Like a domestic house cat, he curled up in the sun, and purred himself to sleep.

As he left for inner worlds, he was thinking to himself how free he felt, how content: how happy.

"That's good" said a voice from somewhere behind him. The great tiger leapt up and spun around to see this intruder. But there was nothing there. He growled his deepest most threatening growl. But nothing appeared.

"You don't have to be afraid of ME." a voice said from somewhere. "I am the fairy who lives in this meadow, and I must say I have never seen anything the likes of YOU before." From behind the colour of the field emerged this exquisite creature with long wings, and a slight body. She was a little taller than the tiger, and had a sense of light shining from her. Never in his born days had the Tiger seen anything like this, and he was entranced.

In his world beauty was in the taste of prey, in hunting, in sleeping. It was never found in anything else, but his world had turned and with no warning Cupid set loose the bow. The Tiger became completely helpless before this fairy. A different sort of hunger took hold of him, a need to have something of this creature for himself. Yes, the Tiger had fallen in Love.

The arrow had struck hard, and the mighty beast was completely, and utterly smitten. Perhaps the fairy felt the same way, you cannot be sure with the Fey creatures, but she did seem to enjoy the presence of this magnificent beast. They sat in the meadow for days while she asked him all manner of questions about the world he came from.

She seemed fascinated by the way he described hunting. Obviously, the art of killing was something he took entirely for granted, but to the fairy it was a truly remarkable thing. "You chase down the deer, and eat them! Do you think the deer are afraid of you?"

"Of course they are." Tiger said proudly. "All creatures are afraid of me, because I eat them." He smiled his teeth at her, and she stepped back. "But I would never eat you."

"Well, that's good to hear," she said.

They talked and walked and played, discovering each other. Fairy showed Tiger the scent of flowers, and all the gentle things he had never known. Slowly the Tiger started to really love this meadow as he did the fairy. Each day they carried on from the last, and each night they slept, she snuggled up against his fur, and he feeling her breath tingle his nose.

Not once did he feel the pang of hunger, or the need to hunt, or even the wish to return to his jungle. Tiger was deeply, hugely content in a way that perhaps no Tiger had ever known before.

Yet one day, when they were playing, Tiger accidentally let a claw slip, and ripped a slice through one of the fairies wings. She stopped, all joy gone from her voice, and she said "You try to harm me?"

"I am truly sorry," said the Tiger "My claw slipped. I promise it won't happen again."

"Never?" the fairy said with one eyebrow raised, as she mended her wing with a spell. "Trust is everything Tiger. If I cannot trust you, there can be no bridge between our worlds. Do you understand?"

Tiger felt a bitter taste in his mouth. He apologised once more, and the fairy accepted it was a mistake, and forgave him. Soon they went back to their talks and their play as if nothing had happened, yet for the Tiger he knew that one day another claw might slip out. For the first time he realised he was not being entirely natural here. He realised that his contentment had a cost!

Even so, he was prepared to pay this small inconvenience. However, despite all good intentions far worse was to occur. He had never meant to, he never wanted to, but one night he had been dreaming: He was chasing down a tasty looking rabbit, and just as he went to snap his jaws over its body he awoke with a scream beside him.

"Tiger!" shouted the Fairy, "You just tried to EAT me! How could you?"

Tiger woke with a shock. He must have snapped at the Fairy in his dream. "I am so sorry. I was chasing a rabbit in my dream, and I was snapping at it, not you. I am so sorry" and he was! But this did not change the reality of things.

"I see," said the Fairy. Something had changed in her eyes, something terrible had happened. "Tiger, the truth is simple. You are a Tiger, I am a Fairy. We may love each other, but the reality is that I have to remain aware at all times, even in sleep, because you may bite me. You have already torn a wing, and you almost ate me just then.

"Nothing can change what we are, Tiger." And with sad eyes, the fairy seemed to fade back into the colour of the meadow from where she had come.

She was gone. Gone! Tiger was distraught, and howled out "No! I can change. I don't want to hurt you, I don't want to lose you! Come back."

A voice flowed from the ethers around him, "Tiger, for you to change would be for you to become tame. I could not bear to watch your brilliant eyes lose their fierce sparkle, or watch you forget how to hunt and forget what you truly are. You must be what you are, my friend."

Tiger knew the Fairy was saying farewell. He leapt forward to try and stop her leaving but all he caught was a brilliant flash of sunlight where his Fairy love had once been. The spell had been broken, his heart howled with sorrow, and his belly growled with hunger.

A deer appeared on the edge of the clearing, and instinct took over. Tiger ran after it, feeling the power of his legs, sensing the sharpness of his vision, smelling the taste of fear in his quarry. He bounded after the fleeing creature chasing it down after a short hunt. But seeing it there as he closed its jaws around its neck, Tiger felt a pang of regret.

It was not the same anymore. Something deep within him had changed. Hunger decided what he must do, but the thrill of biting had gone. He felt for the deer, but ate it anyway, and it felt good to have food in his belly. How long had he lived in that strange dream he had? What had he seen there: A Fairy?

Already the beast had begun to forget his one great love. It is not that he is fickle, it is just that he is a Tiger. Yet even so, things were different. Now when Tiger met the snake, it seemed impossibly vain as it bragged about what it had killed. Leopards just seemed dull and uninteresting, and rather foolish. His own life seemed pointless and vaguely selfish. So it was with discontent that Tiger started each day.

Life held no surprises for him, the flavour of victory seemed less sweet as he tracked down yet another animal to eat, and the bitter remembrance of a thing called Love seemed to be a poison in his veins. His only relief came in his world of Dreams.

And so, Tiger spent more and more time asleep in the sunlight, lost to this world. Even the animals he hunted could feel the difference in him, and then one day the most remarkable thing happened: Tiger shed a tear.

It all came flooding back. He remembered the time with the Fairy in that forgotten meadow. He recalled the long walks and the talks and the play. He saw how he had torn her wing, how he had almost eaten her, and for the first time he felt a bitter taste of regret.

Yet that morning when he awoke the dream had faded. Tiger woke again each morning, again and again, wondering what was haunting him, not knowing what was wrong.

In a meadow not so far away, that same morning would find a Fairy collecting the dew, speaking to the bees, whispering her love to the birds and flowers, and at the same time thinking about her dearest Tiger, the one who had loved her.

She had loved him for his wild spirit, yet that same love, in the end, would have blunted his teeth, dulled his reflexes, and sapped his spirit. He would have lost everything she adored about him.

She sighed, for there was no answer to this riddle. It was a Paradox of Love, that both natures, the dangerous Tiger and the gentle Fairy, could be completed by, yet at the same time opposed to, each other.

Bones of Contention

I had come to Adelaide after living in the heart of Sydney for over a decade. Ostensibly, it was to help a friend start a magazine, but in truth, I needed a change. But my Sydney friends were mystified. Why would anyone leave Sydney to go to Adelaide? It was a massive social faux pas, akin to committing emotional suicide.

"But WHY?" they asked, looking at me as if I were mad. I decided to short circuit the never ending questions by simply saying, "It's because I can get a cappuccino for just One Dollar." There were no further questions. No Sydney-sider could argue THAT sort of logic.

I moved to a very nice sea-side apartment, an older arrangement, but entirely comfortable and with a fantastic view. I was on nodding acquaintance with the others in the small block, but I really had little time to stop and chat. My hours were long and I was effectively running two jobs, and also writing through the evenings. I had left the 1904 Remington, and updated to a 1960's portable typewriter.

However, one Sunday I was in the open carport fixing my motorbike when one of the young fellows that lived in the block, a man called Paul, popped out and asked if I would like a lemonade. "How nice" I thought to myself, and gratefully accepted. We got to chatting, and this sparked off one of the oddest conversations of my life.

"You type a lot." said Paul, making the comment both a statement and question combined. "I hear you, you see. The sound bounces through your window, and into my room." This was 1989, well before computers, and the regular tip tip tip of the typewriter would carry in the still night air. I miss that sound.

"Yes, I am a writer," I replied.

"Oh, and what do you write?"

"Many things. Commercial work, such as I am doing now involves me putting together a booklet on basic exercises to use when working out with a gym, one made in this city. But otherwise I am writing stories, books, that sort of stuff."

Paul looked very interested, then asked. "Could you type something up for me?"

Why do people who do not type for a living ever understand, typing is hard work. "I really don't do typist work, my friend. You will find typist notices up for people who like to do that sort of thing."

He looks rather intently at me. "it's ... ah .. confidential. Legal stuff that I really don't want other eyes looking at, but I felt I could trust you. I am willing to pay! Look, don't say yes or no, why don't you come in and get to know my flat mate, Michael, and myself. Paul is my name." He reached out to shake my hand.

More to be sociable, but also because I had had enough of the bike for the present, I agreed. I must say, there was no indicator at that point that my friend was stark, raving mad. Both he and his friend seemed so perfectly normal that such this thought had never even crossed my mind.

Paul made a cup of tea, and introduced Michael, saying to his friend with a knowing look, "He's a professional writer you know."

After some small talk, I got to the point. "Really, your own solicitor is usually the one who types up the legal documents. I am not sure why you would want me to do this."

Both flat mates looked long and hard at each other. Paul finally spoke, saying, "It's a very confidential matter, one that is both legal and spiritual. We both picked you for being a spiritual man, and felt it was no coincidence that God brought you to stay here beside us."

Even now, no specific alarm bells were ringing. It was the late 1980's and people used the term "spiritual" like you or I may say "tidy" or "clean". I was indeed working on a New Age magazine and such talk was quite common. "Even so," I replied. "Can you give me some sort of outline. How many pages? What sort of content? What is the time frame? This sort of thing."

"You would need to swear a vow of secrecy, not to tell another living soul." NOW the alarm bell finally went off. "Oh?" I asked, "It's that important? They both nodded gravely. "Well, I am happy to keep things confidential, but I would need to know a little bit about what I am supposed to keep confidential before I could agree to this."

This must have made sense, and Paul asks, "But if you agree to do this, you will agree to keep it strictly confidential?" I nodded that I could, knowing even then that there was little chance of me proceeding. Yet my curiosity had me now, and I really wanted to know what it was all about.

"I used to work for ... *Eveready*." His pause, and stressing of the word Eveready was obviously to impress on me how important this was. "There was an industrial accident. Some of the acid used in the battery making was spilt." There was another significant pause. "The acid has contaminated me. It has gone through my skin, and destroyed my bones. This is what I am suing about."

"If you have had contact with hydroflouric acid, it is fairly straight forward, Paul. There's no secrecy in how it affect the nerves and bones." I suggested. "It wasn't that sort of acid," he said "just the normal acid battery. It has eaten away my bones."

I laughed a little. "Obviously, if you bones are eaten away, the first question is going to be *'What is holding you up?'* " I half laughed, but it was no laughing matter to these lads. Paul looked incredibly serious.

"The Lord Jesus is holding me up!" He announced.

"Praise the Lord! Praise the holy Lord! Bless his name, bless the name of Jesus and the Lord." they BOTH called out in unison.

I knew I must not laugh, but the look on my face was pretty clear, and it triggered off Michael. "You don't believe him, do you? You don't! You do NOT believe him! You don't believe him. You DO NOT believe him." Then he shakes his head, and pulls himself back. "Praise the Lord. I do NOT need the pills. I do NOT need the pills. Praise the Lord."

Then they both continued with a few more Praise the Lord's until Michael settled down. You can imagine what I was thinking.

"Well, supposing that for some reason this IS true," I said earnestly, "surely you have had an X-Ray taken to see what the problem is?"

Paul nodded sagely. "Yes, I have."

"And they showed... What?"

Paul had expected this. "The doctors a good man, but he has been fooled by the devil. He doesn't realize that Satan had painted the bones back in." Both men nodded, the devil was a cunning creature.

"Obviously, your solicitor must have told you there is little chance of this action working?" I asked.

"That's why I need a typist!" Paul said, brightening up. "We need to get this prepared in such a way that he WILL believe!"

Ah yes, it was all clear as mud now. I found a way to gently remove myself, by firstly agreeing with them 100% (I find it does not pay to disagree with madness) then clarifying with them that at my normal rate was fifty five cents a word, and with this likely to run to at least 100 pages, at 500 words per page. That would be two thousand seven hundred and fifty dollars up front, and allowing for corrections and retyping, five to six thousand should do it nicely.

They kindly said they would look at their finances and let me know.

I left on good terms. They were decent people, just completely, and utterly bonkers. I walked away thinking about how two perfectly normal looking people, ones you would happily have a polite conversation with, are in truth, completely insane. Maybe we are ALL just a little insane?

At that time, I thought little more about the matter. Even so, the researcher in me checked, and Olympic Batteries in Adelaide were indeed involved with Eveready.

The year I met Paul and Michael was 1989, the same year that Union Carbide was forced to pay out one of the worlds largest ever industrial fines. There had been 3,787 deaths related to the gas release from the Bhopal factory. It left an estimated 40,000 individuals permanently disabled, maimed, or suffering from serious illness, making it one of the world's worst industrial disasters. Union

Carbide was sued by the Government of India and agreed to an out-of-court settlement of US$470 million.

I had been talking to Paul and Michael a few months prior to this settlement. They would have had no knowledge of this. Further: 1984 was when Paul first started to believe his bones had disappeared: This was the same year as Union Carbide Bhopal accident. and they were the first owners of the Eveready brand. Curious, isn't it?

Yes, they may have been completely mad, but the truth is this: Michael was kept out of the insane asylum because of his love for the Lord. Paul could keep functioning, despite his belief that his bones had vanished, because of his love for the Lord. Without their knowledge at the time, the company that started Eveready WAS indeed responsible for a terrible industrial accident.

Who was truly mad here?

In my humble opinion: The real madness of commercial interests destroying the planet make Paul and Michael's small issues seem positively sane. They do not hurt anyone, and they are kind to other people.

Of course, many years later, as I compile all of this (2015) we have seen how a Global Financial Crisis has crippled the West, and ruined so many lives. The madness that cause it was greed, just like Union Carbide, and so many other huge corporations that put the value of money over the value of people.

Is there any wonder so many people have been driven crazy by the greed and avarice of those who control our society?

I would like to close this book by asking a simple question I was asked many years ago by an interesting fellow most consider somewhat crazy. He found out I was in property development, and looked me right in the eye, and asked:

"I have always wanted to know this, and as you are in the business, perhaps you can answer. Our entire society is wrapped up in the value of what we own, and land is clearly the cornerstone of all ownership. So tell me this: How much does an acre weigh?"

"But more importantly, does it weigh more than the value of the person standing on it?"

These are the real "Bones of Contention", yes?

HELLO PLANET EARTH

Did these stories warm your heart?

By the same author, you can also buy another book based around a series of short stories. This is a truly endearing book about a young man who goes into the wild to escape a society he doesn't understand, and discovers an extraordinarily wise child. Together, they sort out the purpose of each others life.

HELLO PLANET EARTH is an exquisite journey into a world of myth and fascination. It is story telling at its best. The disenchanted young man goes into the wild to find solace, and instead meets an amazing child, who teaches him about the real values he needs to grasp, through the stories of people he has met.

This book will leave you with a sense of joy and happiness.

More info can be found at: laddertothemoon.com.au

Other books by this author:

Ratology: Way of the Un-Dammed

Hello Planet Earth

The Book of Number Series

The Divinity Dice Series

Jerimiah Versus the Grabblesnatch

Water: More Precious than Gold

The Borringbar War

And in the end

the love you take

is equal to the love

you make

Paul McCartney

Are you ready for something different?

From the same writer, we bring you the Divinity Dice Series. This series introduces a series of games that cast dice to give clear answers to questions you ask. It is remarkably accurate, and part of the Pythagorean Tradition made available for the modern person.

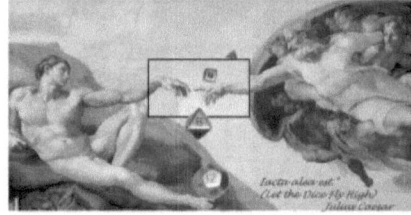

DIVINITY DICE
Play the Dice of the Gods

Cast the Dice of the Gods and allow Life to give you the answers to your deepest, most secret questions

*Iacta alea est."
(Let the Dice Fly High)
Julius Caesar*

Author: *Michael Wallace*

Play the Game of Life
Have Fun with Divinity Dice and discover amazing answers to your deepest questions. Discover how the Ancient Art of Prophecy is still alive in the 21st Century. The Greatest Secret is in Your Hands Right Now!

Divinity Dice is produced under the authority and auspices of the Pythagorean Guild.

These books were written to help the individual grasp how number combinations worked. They provide an easy, practical way to give a natural "Oracular" readings, based on the various castings of the polyhedral dice.

Go to divinitydice.com.au for more information and pricing.

There is also a series of fun workshops available, which allow an individual to grasp the power of the Dice in a group atmosphere.

Absolutely ground breaking stuff!

Without doubt, the most comprehensive books on Dice Divination on the planet.
George Cockcroft, writer of "The Diceman"

Michael Wallace (Raven)

Michael Wallace is a remarkable individual. He is a Master Musician, Master Body Worker, Master Numerologist, Dice Master, Recording Artist, Songwriter, and Publisher. On top of all this he is also a prolific writer with over seventeen titles in print.

Known as "Raven", or what the Hopi describe as the Storm Bringer, he is a catalyst for change and renewal.

Have you ever felt that there was something more?

The ancient art of Divination by Number is an extraordinary study you may wish to contemplate. The author of this book has written a complete course on "how to do" Pythagorean Numerology. In just WEEKS you can learn to discover and understand all the numerical secrets of the Ancient Greeks.

The Book of Number is a series of four books that cover the whole teaching of Number Divination as taught by the Ancient Pythagoreans. This is, available on Amazon or direct from the author. Details are below if you wish to know more.

www.bookofnumber.com.au

For further enquiries and updates go to the official web page at bookofnumber.com.au.

You may also write to info.numberharmonics@gmail.com.

Here you will find all current information on Pythagorean Numerology, as well as where you can find study groups, on line classes and areas of interest to the subject.

www.numberharmonics.org

The original site for the Pythagorean system of Harmonic Healing.

www.divinitydice.com.au

The main site for the study of Dice Divination, based on the
Pythagorean Polyhedral Dice

ISBN: 978-0-9756994-8-5

www.ingramcontent.com/pod-product-compliance
Lightning Source LLC
Chambersburg PA
CBHW032119020726
47494CB00007BA/2149